PRAISE FOR *AVA AND PIP*

2015 Children's Notable Book in the Language Arts

"Weston perfectly captures the complexities of sisterhood…a love letter to language."
—The *New York Times*

"With her engaging voice, jaw-dropping word play, and tales of good people making not-so-good decisions, she casts the perfect spell. A big W-O-W for *Ava and Pip!*"
—Julie Sternberg, author of *Like Pickle Juice on a Cookie*

"Charming! Surprising! Inspiring! A warm and wonderful diary-novel, both funny and important, *Ava and Pip* is Carol Weston's best book yet."
—Karen Bokram, Founding Editor of *Girls' Life*

"…will have fans cheering."
—*Booklist*

"Weston deals with family dynamics and creative challenges in realistic, emotionally honest ways."
—*Shelf Awareness*

Also by Carol Weston

Ava and Taco Cat
Ava XOX

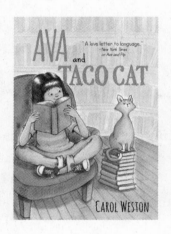

"purrfect"

—*Vanity Fair*

AVA

and

Pip

CAROL WESTON

sourcebooks
jabberwocky

Published by Sourcebooks Jabberwocky, an imprint of Sourcebooks, Inc.
P.O. Box 4410, Naperville, Illinois 60567-4410
(630) 961-3900
Fax: (630) 961-2168
www.jabberwockykids.com

Library of Congress Cataloging-in-Publication Data is on file with the publisher.
Source of Production: Versa Press-USA, East Peoria, IL
Date of Production: July 2016
Run Number: 5007104

Printed and bound in the United States of America.
VP 10 9 8 7 6 5 4

for kids who are shy,
and for kids who are not,

and

in memory of
Christopher Joseph Todd
who loved books

DEAR NEW DIARY,

You won't believe what I just found out.

Fifth grade started today, and my homeroom has three Emilys but only one Ava, so at dinner, I asked Mom and Dad why they named me Ava.

Innocent question, right?

Well, Dad answered: "We like palindromes."

"Palinwhat?" I said.

"Palindromes," Dad replied, passing the salad. "Words that are the same backward and forward."

"Like M-O-M," Mom said.

"And D-A-D," Dad said.

"And P-I-P," Pip chimed. Apparently she knew all about this. "And H-A-N-N-A-H," she added. That's Pip's middle name.

My full name is Ava Elle Wren. When people ask what the L stands for, they expect me to say Lily or Lauren or Louise, but I say, "It's not L, it's E-L-L-E."

I thought about P-I-P, H-A-N-N-A-H, A-V-A, and E-L-L-E, and stared at my parents. "You chose our names because

1

of how they're spelled? Wow." Then I noticed how you spell "wow" (W-O-W).

And suddenly it was as if I saw the whole world—or at least the Whole World of Words—in a brand-new way.

My parents' names are Anna and Bob (A-N-N-A and B-O-B), and they are word nerds.

"Why didn't you tell me before?" I asked.

"You never asked," Dad answered.

"When did you tell Pip?"

"A while ago," Mom said, "when she asked."

Pip looked at me and shrugged. "At least we didn't get named after Nana Ethel."

Pip is twelve—for one more month. She talks at home, but at school, she is extremely shy. Pip was a preemie, which means she was born early. Since our last name is Wren, which is the name of a bird, Mom and Dad sometimes call her Early Bird.

When Pip was little, they worried about her a lot. To tell you the truth, they still worry about her a lot. They also pay way more attention to her than to me. I try not to let it bother me…but it kind of does. I'm only human.

"Guess who was the first woman in the world?" Pip asked.

"Huh?" I replied, then noticed how "huh" (H-U-H) is spelled.

"Eve," Pip said. "E-V-E!"

Dad jumped in. "And guess what Adam said when he saw Eve?"

"What?" I said, totally confused.

"Madam, I'm Adam!" Dad laughed.

"Another palindrome!" Mom explained. "M-A-D-A-M-I-M-A-D-A-M."

"A whole sentence can be a palindrome?" I asked.

"Yes." Dad pointed to Mom's plate. "Like, 'Ma has a ham!'"

Pip spelled that out: "M-A-H-A-S-A-H-A-M."

I put down my fork, looked from my S-I-S to my M-O-M to my P-O-P, and started wondering if other people's families are as nutty as mine. Or is mine extra nutty? Like, chunky-peanut-butter nutty?

A-V-A

RIDICULOUSLY LATE

DEAR DIARY,

It's wayyy past my bedtime, and I'm hoping Mom and Dad won't barge in and tell me to turn off my light. But something's been keeping me awake.

After dinner, Pip and I played Battleship. We usually like sinking each other's carriers, cruisers, submarines, destroyers, and battleships. It's fun. She'll say, for instance, "B-8." And I'll say, "I can't B-8 because I'm 10!" Or I'll say, "I-1." And she'll say, "No, you didn't! The game isn't over!"

Tonight I was about to sink Pip's last ship when I said, "I-4." But Pip said, "I-quit."

"You can't quit!" I protested.

"I can and I did!" she said and stomped off to her room.

That made me so mad! I hate when my big sister acts like a little sister! I hate when she's a sore loser!

Once, after a teacher conference, I overheard Mom and Dad talking about Pip's "social issues" and how they wish they could help her "come out of her shell."

Well, sometimes I wish I could take a hammer and break Pip's "shell" into a million zillion pieces. What if she *never* comes out? What if she grows up to be a sore loser quitter with no friends and a hundred cats and only me to talk to?

Thinking about Pip drives me crazy. Here's why: I always end up feeling mad at her *and* bad for her all at the same time!

The problem is that sometimes her problems turn into *my* problems. Like when I have to clean up after a game of Battleship or Clue or Monopoly by myself. Or when I have friends over and Pip doesn't come out of her room. Or when I walk into the kitchen and Mom and Dad suddenly go all quiet because they were in the middle of talking about her.

I know Pip isn't shy on purpose, but it still gets me mad.

AVA, ARRRGGGHHH

DEAR DIARY,

Whenever I start a new diary—like I'm doing this week—I end up accidentally writing something totally embarrassing that I would never want *anyone* to see. Then I put my pen down and bury the diary in my dresser drawer.

So far in my life, I've started seven diaries and finished zero. It's like there's a dead diary graveyard underneath my underwear!

Today in language arts, Mrs. Lemons asked us what we read this summer. Well, my family reads big books for fun—they even reread and *reread* them. But long books intimidate me.

Long words (like "gigantic" and "intimidate") don't scare me, just long books.

Here's how I pick books:

1. I look at the front and back covers.
2. I check to see if it's about a regular kid with normal problems (not superscary or supernatural problems).
3. I read the first page so I can hear the "voice" and how it sounds.
4. I peek at the last page to see how long it is.

If there are too many pages, forget it, I put the book back.

In *short*, I like *short* books.

Mrs. Lemons also asked us when we read. A lot of kids said, "Before bed," but one girl, Riley, said, "On the bus," and one boy, Chuck, said, "If I read on the bus, I'd barf. I get bus sick."

Mrs. Lemons said, "How about you, Ava?"

"Sometimes I read before bed," I said, "but sometimes I write." I did not add that when I was little, I thought I was a great writer because I could write my whole name before Elizabeth and Katherine and Stephanie could write theirs. (Pip burst my bubble by pointing out that Ava has only three letters and theirs each have nine.)

"It's good to keep a journal," Mrs. Lemons said. "And, Ava, your handwriting is excellent."

"It used to be terrible," I confessed. "In first grade, Mrs. Quintano said I didn't even hold my pencil right."

I don't know why I blurted that out except that it was true. In first grade, I erased more than I wrote, and I collected erasers— pink rectangle ones and colorful ones shaped like cupcakes and rainbows and sushi.

Now I like pens more than pencils, and I have a favorite pen. It's silver with black ink and is the kind you click, not the kind with a cap. Dad bought it for me at the Dublin Writers Museum, and I am using it right now. I think of it as my magic pen, and I like to imagine that it has special powers and that I can write anything I want with it—anything at all!

Dad is a real writer. He's a playwright—which is spelled playwright, not *playwrite*. He works at home writing plays and tutoring students.

Mom has a regular job—she runs the office of a vet named Dr. Gross who is more grumpy than gross.

At the end of class, Mrs. Lemons asked one last question. She said, "What do you want to be when you grow up?" Everyone said things like "President," "Ballerina," "Doctor," "Actor," "Fireman," "Rock star," "Comedian," "Chef," and "Fifth-grade teacher." Maybelle (my best friend) said, "Astronaut," and Chuck said, "Championship boxer."

I was the only person who said, "I don't know."

AVA WITH A FUZZY FUTURE

DEAR DIARY,

We had the first spelling test of fifth grade today and I got a 100. So at dinner, I said, "I got a 100 on a spelling test."

Dad said, "Great," but I could tell he was mostly concentrating on cutting up the chicken. Mom didn't really hear me either. She was talking about an operation Dr. Gross did on a dog that ate a rock.

I decided to tell a dog joke, so I said,

"Question: What does a dog eat at the movies?
Answer: Pup corn!"

I was going to point out that P-U-P is a palindrome and that popcorn goes P-O-P P-O-P P-O-P, but since no one laughed, I didn't.

And okay, I realize my joke was lame, but couldn't Mom and Dad have laughed a little?

Sometimes it feels like they don't quite see me. Or hear me. It's like I'm not even at the table.

Maybe *I* should go eat a rock.

A

DEAR DIARY,

Pip was on the sofa with her freckly nose in a book. "You read that book last week!" I said.

She said that when she first reads a book, it's to find out what happens, but when she rereads a book, it's like being with a friend.

Here's what I did not say: "You need *real* friends!"

Instead, I went to the basement and opened a few old boxes. In one, I found a bag of plastic animals that Pip and I used to play with. I picked out a lion cub and took it to the kitchen and put it in a jar and covered it with corn oil. Why? So it would be a lion in oil.

Get it? L-I-O-N-I-N-O-I-L is a palindrome! And I came up with it all by myself!

I put the jar on the windowsill and am waiting for M-O-M and D-A-D and P-I-P to find it and figure it out. They are going to love my little L-I-O-N-I-N-O-I-L!

AVA IN ANTICIPATION

DEAR DIARY,

Our librarian, Mr. Ramirez, knows I'm big on words. "Ava, you like to write," he said. "You should enter the Misty Oaks Library story contest."

"I don't think so," I said.

"Why not?"

"Because I won't win."

He frowned. "Well, you definitely won't win if you don't enter. Why not give it a shot?"

I wanted to say, "A shot? I'm not a doctor." But I just listened as he explained that the story had to be four hundred words, the title had to include the name of a living creature, and the deadline was October 12.

"I'll think about it," I said. And I have been. A lot. Maybe too much.

If I won a library contest, Mom and Dad would be proud of me for sure, so I'm trying to come up with ideas.

Like, what if I write about two crazy cats that are losing their minds? I could name them Nan (N-A-N) and Viv (V-I-V) and call the story:

SENILE FELINES

Get it? S-E-N-I-L-E-F-E-L-I-N-E-S is a palindrome!
Pretty smart, right?
>^..^< >^..^<

A-V-A A-V-A

DEAR DIARY,

I read what I wrote yesterday, and omg, what a stupid idea!

Good thing no one ever sees what I write in here except me.

To tell you the truth, I'm getting tempted to bury this diary underneath my underwear!

The reason I came up with the crazy cats idea is that Mom is always saying how sad it is when old pets get "put down." Yesterday, some lady realized that her beloved cat, Whiskers, had gotten so rickety, he could no longer drink or eat and that "his time had come."

Mom says the worst part of her job is when a person walks in with a pet and walks out without one. The second worst is when someone gets the pet back, good as new, and Mom hands them a bill for a thousand dollars, and the person faints on the floor. (That almost happened to the lady with the rock-eating dog.)

Anyway, instead of writing any sad sagas (S-A-G-A-S) about ancient cats, I might write about glamorous rats: star rats (S-T-A-R-R-A-T-S). Who knows? With my magic pen, I might even win!

X-O-X
A-V-A

9-9
(A NUMBER PALINDROME)

DEAR DIARY,

So far, no one has spotted my L-I-O-N-I-N-O-I-L.

AVA, ACTUALLY

DEAR DIARY,

This might sound dumb and immature, but I'm sitting in bed crying. Two little drops just fell on *you*!

At dinner, I said, "I got another 100 in spelling." I wasn't expecting a bunch of high-fives or a confetti parade or for them to dance around the room or phone Nana Ethel. But couldn't they have said, "Way to go"? Or, if they wanted to be nutty, "Yay, Ava, Yay" (Y-A-Y-A-V-A-Y-A-Y) or "Atta girl" (A-T-T-A girl)?

Dad said, "Ava, you're on a roll," and Mom said, "Now please pass me a roll." Dad laughed at her not-that-funny joke, then Mom and Dad and Pip started talking about rolls and Pip's art class and a calico kitten named Fuzz Ball who got hit by a car and operated on and now has just three legs but still scampers around just fine.

And I can see how all of that is wayyy more interesting than a 100 in spelling, but I still wish that what mattered to me mattered to them.

After dinner, I remembered my palindrome project, so I said, "Hey, did anybody notice my little lion?"

Mom, Dad, and Pip stared at me blankly, so I hopped up to show them. But it wasn't on the windowsill! I looked all around, and it was *nowhere* to be found! I came back and said, "I put a lion cub in a jar next to the cactus." Dad and Pip looked at me like I had three noses, but Mom said, "Oh, sweetie, I threw it out. I thought it was garbage." And she didn't even apologize!

I stomped upstairs to write in you, but I left my magic pen in the living room and I didn't want to go back down, so now I'm writing with an old pencil. That's how I feel anyway: like a stubby yellow pencil covered with teeth marks with a worn-down eraser and a broken point that no one even cares about.

AVA FEELING AWFUL

Dear Diary,

One nice thing about keeping a diary is that it never interrupts or changes the subject or thinks your jokes aren't funny or that you're boasting or whining. And it's not a writing contest, so there's no pressure. A diary just lets you be honest. And I appreciate that.

I also appreciate that Dad made a big Irish breakfast with eggs, sausages, baked beans, mushrooms, and scones.

AVA THE APPRECIATIVE

Saturday ~~Day~~ Night

Dear Diary,

Maybelle invited me to dinner, but I was with our neighbors Lucia and Carmen. They're fourth-grade twins, and they don't dress exactly the same, but they always wear the same color. Today it was pink.

Maybelle said they could come too, so Dad drove the three of us over.

At dinner, which was a cookout, Maybelle's parents asked me lots of friendly questions. Maybelle told them about the writing contest and even said, "Ava can spell anything!"

Maybelle's dad said, "Spell *anything*!"

I said, "A-N-Y-T-H-I-N-G," and everyone laughed.

After dinner, we all went for a walk. We didn't need flashlights because the moon was almost full. When it was just me and Maybelle, I told her about my oily lion palindrome project and how my mom threw it out. Maybelle looked sad for me, but then Lucia and Carmen caught up with us so she changed the subject. She said, "I like the moon more than the sun."

"What do you mean?" Carmen said.

"You can't look directly at the sun," Maybelle explained. "But you can look at the moon all you want. And it changes!"

"I like when it's bright and there are no clouds," Lucia chimed in. "Like tonight."

"Moon shadows are cooler than sun shadows," Maybelle added.

Well, I started waving my arms in the air, and my shadow started waving its arms on the ground. It was all stretched out in front of me, long and skinny. Maybelle, Lucia, and Carmen started waving their arms too, and soon we were all jumping up and down—and so were our long skinny shadows.

Maybelle said, "The moon is 240,000 miles away."

Lucia looked surprised, but I'm used to Maybelle being a math wonk and coming out with random facts.

"Another thing I like," Maybelle said, "is that you don't have to worry about moonscreen or moonglasses."

"Hey, I brought moonscreen!" I blurted. "Smell!" I squeezed a pretend blob onto everyone's palm.

"Lemon lavender!" Maybelle said.

"Gingerbread spice!" Lucia said.

"Strawberry shortcake!" Carmen said.

"Grape with a hint of honeysuckle," I said, and then at the exact same time, we all went "Mmm!" (M-M-M).

"I also brought moonglasses!" I said and handed out pretend pairs.

"I'm putting mine on top of my head," Maybelle said. "The movie star way."

"Me too!" Lucia said.

"Me three!" Carmen said.

"Me four!" I said, and we laughed.

"What's so funny?" Maybelle's dad asked.

"The man in the moon!" Maybelle said, and we all kept walking and laughing with our moonglasses on top of our heads, in the dark but not-too-dark.

I wish we could have walked for hours.

And I wish my family liked to laugh and have fun together.

AVA IN THE MOONLIGHT

DEAR DIARY,

I told Mom how fun last night was, and instead of saying, "That's nice," she said, "You should have invited Pip." Well, that made me mad because it's not my fault that Pip doesn't have real friends!

AVA IN THE MORNING

IN THE LIBRARY

DEAR DIARY,

Mr. Ramirez just asked how my story was coming along.

My story? What story? I didn't tell him that I don't have a character or a plot or even a first sentence.

At least I have a magic pen.

O-X-O
A-V-A

Dear Diary,

After school, I went to Dr. Gross's and waited for Mom. She was really busy, so I had to sit in the waiting room. After a while, I said, "I'm bored."

Mom said, "Shhh."

She hates when I say, "I'm bored."

I hate when she says, "Shhh."

I also hate being quiet. Pip is the Queen of Quiet. She's even quiet when she goes up and down stairs while I, according to Mom, sound like "a herd of elephants."

In school, Pip can go a whole day without saying five words. Last year, Lacey, a loudmouth girl with thick bangs and thick eyeliner, teased her and called her "Pipsqueak." It made Pip even quieter!

I don't know why Pip is so quiet. She just is. It's like she has permanent stage fright—and she's not even an actress.

I realize it must be hard for her, but does she realize that it's hard for me too?

Pip and I don't look that much alike (I have longish brown

hair and brown eyes and no freckles, and she has medium red hair and green eyes and tons of freckles). We also don't act alike (I talk fast and a lot, and she barely talks at all, and I write a lot, and she draws a lot). To be honest, I'm glad most people don't know we're related. It can be embarrassing when kids find out we're sisters. They say, "You mean the short pretty girl who never talks?" or "You mean the weird girl who eats lunch by herself?"

Pip isn't weird. She just has no life. Hardly anyone besides me even knows that deep down, she's normal. And nice—well, except when she's bratty.

One thing I like about having a big sister is she tells me stuff about when I was little. Like, she says I used to call "marshmallows" "marshmelons." And once I had a tick on me and called it a "ticket." And once I got us both in trouble because instead of a lemonade stand, I wanted to have a flower shop, so I cut all of Mom and Dad's tulips so we could sell them. (Oops!)

Anyway, while I was waiting in the waiting room, I started thinking about how Dr. Gross does *cat* scans on *cat*s and *lab* tests on *Labs* (Labrador retrievers). And I came up with an unbelievable four-word palindrome: Step On No Pets (S-T-E-P-O-N-N-O-P-E-T-S).

I was really proud of myself, and I told Mom I was going to make them a sign. I even started digging markers out of her drawer. But Mom said, "Not now, Ava! Can't you see I'm trying to finish up?"

I said, "Okay." But it was *not* okay. It was not one bit okay! In fact, it made *me* feel stepped on.

At five, Mom made sure all the animals were happy. There were lots of cats and dogs, two birds, two hamsters, one ferret, and a green basilisk lizard that would probably be walking on water if it weren't stuck in a tank at Dr. Gross's. Mom and I locked up, and I asked where the lizard came from. She said Central America and started telling me about a famous palindrome about a Central American waterway: "A man. A plan. A canal. Panama" (A-M-A-N-A-P-L-A-N-A-C-A-N-A-L-P-A-N-A-M-A).

"H-U-H," I said, and wondered how many other kids have word-nerd families and silent siblings and moms who sometimes seem like they care more about other people's pets than their own daughter.

AVA ALL ALONE?

9/19
Saturday, bedtime

Dear Diary,

I found a two-word note from Pip on my desk. It said: "Wanna talk?"

I do, but her lights are off, and she gets mad when I wake her up.

AVA IN SUSPENSE

9/20
AFTERNOON

Dear Diary,

Pip and I were on the floor in her room doing Word Scrambles. I asked what she wanted to talk about, but she said she changed her mind.

I said, "That's not fair!"

She shrugged.

Dad shouted up from the kitchen, "Who wants a Sunday sundae?"

A Sunday sundae is my favorite dessert, so I shouted, "Meeeee!" and ran downstairs.

While Dad was sprinkling nuts on our ice cream, I told him about the contest. Big mistake! He said I should definitely submit a story.

I told him my ideas about S-E-N-I-L-E-F-E-L-I-N-E-S and S-T-A-R-R-A-T-S.

He asked, "Does the 'living creature' have to be a palindrome?"

I said, "No," and started feeling small.

"Then think big," he said. "You'll come up with something. You have a facility with language."

"H-U-H?" I asked palindromically.

"A way with words." He smiled. "Be patient. You'll find your voice."

Dad says the best writers have a "voice," which means their words flow naturally, and you can recognize their style, and it's almost as if you can "hear" them reading to you.

I wish I had a "voice."

I wish I had a subject!

I guess I should be glad I can write about anything. Anything at all. Anything in the whole wide world! Anything alive!

But what should I write about? Princesses or presidents? Lions or lionfish? Friends or enemies? Frenemies??

Blank pages can be scary.

And I'm *not* patient.

"A way with words"? Right now I feel like shouting: "Away with words!"

AVA THE ANXIOUS

DEAR DIARY,

Pip's door was open a crack, so I said, "Pip, c'mon, tell me the thing you were going to tell me."

"It's not a thing," she said. "It's a person." Then she said she was going to bed, but that tomorrow we could do some more Word Scrambles.

AVA IN MYSTERY

CAROL WESTON

DEAR DIARY,

Not only have I not *found* my voice, I've *lost* my pen!! The silver one Dad brought me back from Ireland!

Last night when we were running errands, Dad said that even though Ireland is not a big country, four Irish writers got the biggest prize a writer can get: the Nobel Prize.

I couldn't bring myself to tell him that I lost his—*my*—prize pen.

Until now, I hadn't even told *you*, my diary. I just stopped writing for a week. But *not* writing did *not* make me feel better.

Well, here I am, back again. I'm using a plain pen with the name of a boring bank on it. And I'm worried that I'll never be able to write anything good again—let alone anything prize-worthy.

AVA, AVERAGE

9/29
ALMOST DINNERTIME

DEAR DIARY,

I barged into Pip's room and said, "I know two transportation palindromes."

Pip said, "You have to learn to knock!"

I went back out and knocked, and Pip said, "Who's there?" so I said, "Ava," and then barged in and said, "I know two transportation palindromes."

She looked up and said, "K-A-Y-A-K and R-A-C-E-C-A-R. Duh."

I sighed and sat on her bed. "What are you doing?" I asked. The answer was pretty obvious because there were pants and tops everywhere.

"Trying on clothes."

"Aren't you going to tell me your secret?"

"No."

"Pleeeease." She didn't answer, so I said, "Just answer me this: is the 'person' a boy?" Pip blushed a little, so I said, "I knew it!"

She got pinker and said, "Don't tell anyone, okay?"

"Okay," I said.

"Not a word!" she said.

"Not a P-E-E-P!" I agreed. "But, Pip, if you have a crush, you have to tell me who it is."

"No, I don't," she said. "That stays secret."

AVA AGAIN

10/01 (1-0-0-1)
BEDTIME

DEAR DIARY,

What if I'm stuck? What if I have writer's block? I have no pen, no voice, no words, *no no*thing! And my story is due in eleven days.

Dad says I'm too young to have writer's block. He got it once after a theater critic wrote a bad review of one of his plays. Dad had worked hard, and the actors had worked hard, and the director and stage manager and costume and set and lighting designers had all worked hard, and then a reporter sat down and didn't like the show and said so. People stopped coming, and the show closed early, and it was sad for Dad.

For a while, he started moping instead of writing.

That was no fun for him—or for us, either!

It helped a little when Dad's brother, Uncle Patrick, sent a note that said,

"The play was a great success but the audience was a disaster."

Oscar Wilde

Dad taped it on the wall by his desk, and it's still there.

I wish someone would write me an encouraging note.

Today, Mom and Pip started planning Pip's birthday. She invited six seventh-graders to a slumber party. I think Mom's hoping the party will fix Pip's "social issues."

Here's what I love about slumber parties:

1. Staying up late
2. Raiding the refrigerator
3. Sleeping in sleeping bags
4. Doing Mad Libs

This will be Pip's first real slumber party ever! She usually tries hard to stay off everyone's radar (R-A-D-A-R). I mean, if someone next to her sneezes, I bet she doesn't even say, "Bless you."

It's as if Pip thinks people will bite—like the mean dogs Dr. Gross sometimes has to take care of. The ones that when they're hungry, the assistants open the cage door just a crack, put in the food really fast, and shut the door again before they snarl or nip or worse.

For Pip's party, Mom offered to bring party pets, including a one-eyed owl from the wildlife refuge center.

Pip said, "Mom, I'm not in second grade!"

I think Mom forgets how old Pip is because Pip doesn't act her age and I'm two and a half inches taller. (We just got checkups.)

Unlike me, Pip never keeps a diary. She's not a writer; she's a drawer.

Wait, that makes her sound like a piece of furniture! I mean, she's an artist—she likes to draw and sketch.

Questions:

Do artists ever get artist's block?

And *do* I have writer's block?

At least I have you. When I write in you, it's not for a prize or review or grade or anything.

I've decided to stop thinking about the dumb contest.

Who cares about it anyway? Even if I entered, I'd probably lose. I'm excellent at losing things.

AVA, BLOCKED

DEAR DIARY,

I got a 100 on a spelling test but didn't even mention it.

AVA AGAIN (AGAIN)

Dear Diary,

Yesterday, I asked Maybelle if she ever noticed that her name starts with *Maybe*.

"*Maybe*," *Maybe*lle said and laughed. I think she must have, but then I'd never noticed that my family's names are all palindromic.

Last night, Maybelle *slept over*, and this morning we *overslept*. She was supposed to be at a soccer game at ten sharp, but she forgot!

She's lucky—her mom didn't even get mad.

Today I wanted to ask my mom to help me think up story ideas, but she was busy with Pip. They were ordering helium balloons and a gigantic strawberry cake that says "Happy Birthday, Pip." Now they're talking about what to put in the goody bags and what kind of pancakes to make on Sunday—blueberry or chocolate chip.

To tell you the truth, I'm getting sick of the whole subject. I know they don't want Pip's party to be a dud (D-U-D) and they want it to be really fun, or at least fun enuf (F-U-N-E-N-U-F). But Mom never makes a big deal about my birthdays.

And that's not fair. She's my mom too!

AVA, AN AFTERTHOUGHT?

10/5
AFTER SCHOOL

DEAR DIARY,

Pip came home from school *sobbing*. During first period, a girl told her that something came up and she couldn't go to Pip's party. During second period, a second girl told her the same thing. During third period, a third girl also said her plans had changed. In gym, when even Isabel, who lives three houses away, offered a lame excuse, Pip made her tell her what was going on. Isabel did, but that got Pip even more upset.

What she found out is that this new kid, Bea, who has long straight blond hair, is having a boy-girl party on Saturday—the first boy-girl party of seventh grade!

Pip said it wasn't fair that everyone was going to Bea's party when she'd known them longer and invited them first. Then she ran to the girls' room and hid out and ended up being late to science, and her teacher was giving a pop (P-O-P) quiz, so he gave her a zero.

Poor Pip! She's never gotten a zero before. She usually gets nothing but straight As because she's so smart and hardworking (even though she never participates).

Now she's in her bedroom doing an extra-credit science project to make up for the zero. She just came out with puffy eyes and said she hates the new girl's guts.

I said, "Me too."

Pip called Mom at work, and Mom offered to call Isabel's parents or the new girl's parents, but Pip begged her not to and said it would only make everything worse.

I feel so bad for Pip. Even though I was getting sick of hearing about her party, I never thought she'd have to cancel it!

I wish I could help.

AVA THE ANGRY

I don't know what to write!

I still don't know what to write!!

I STILL don't know what to write!!!

DEAR DIARY,

I told Mrs. Lemons I have writer's block and asked if it's curable. She said, "Ava, sometimes you just have to get out of your own way. I know you can write a wonderful story—no—lots of wonderful stories!"

I mumbled, "Thank you."

Chuck, the boy who wants to be a boxer and who gets bus sick, added, "Ava, you stress out too much. Who even cares if you submit a dumb story or not?"

I mumbled, "I do."

AVA, IN HER OWN WAY

DEAR DIARY,

Yippee! I have a story idea! And it might help Pip feel better too!

Wish me luck. I have only three days.

Dad and I went to the copy shop to buy paper, and I confessed to him that I lost my pen. Dad didn't get mad at me because he could tell I was already mad at myself. He said that even great writers lose their pens from time to time and offered to buy me a new one.

I went up to the display and tried out scented pens and glittery pens and fountain pens and pens with feather tops and pens with gold ink and pens with erasable ink. Finally I picked out a pen with turquoise ink. It's cool, but it does not feel magical and obviously does not have "the luck of the Irish."

On the way home, Dad told me the names of the four Irish writers who won the Nobel Prize: Yeats, Shaw, Beckett, and Heaney. He said I should read their books someday. I said, "Are they short?"

Dad laughed. The book he is now rereading is a thousand pages long! It's called *Ulysses* and is about one day in the life of one person in Ireland.

Dad started talking about "sloppy copy" (messy first drafts) and said, "Writers have to write and rewrite till they get it right." He also said writers have to let their words "sit and marinate" so they can return to them with "fresh eyes."

When Dad is in the middle of writing a play, he sometimes invites actors to come over to read the lines out loud in our dining room. This helps him figure out what works and what doesn't. Sometimes the actors come back a month later to read the same old play with brand-new changes.

Well, I can't let my words sit and marinate! I barely have enough time to "cook" them up in the first place!

Speaking of cooking, for dinner, we ordered in Chinese. (Actually, we *ordered* in English, but we got Chinese food.) Dessert was pineapple rings and fortune cookies, and I am taping my fortune here:

Hard work without talent is a shame,
but talent without hard work is a tragedy.

Was that message meant for me?? I haven't been working very hard lately.

This weekend, while stupid Bea has her stupid boy-girl party and Pip quietly turns thirteen, I plan to write and write.

Here's my title:

STING OF THE QUEEN BEE

Get it? "Queen Bee" as in *buzz buzz* and "Queen Bee" as in popular girl. That's a homonym. "Bee" can also mean contest as in "spelling bee." And of course "bee" sounds like "Bea," as in mean-awful-new-seventh-grade-girl.

Titles are my specialty.

AVA THE AMBITIOUS

DEAR DIARY,

I spent all afternoon writing, and it felt as if I were in another world. I totally lost track of time! Suddenly Mom said, "Get dressed," because we were going to the Kahiki for Pip's birthday.

The Kahiki is Pip's and my favorite restaurant. It is Polynesian and has big bubbling aquariums, flaming spicy meatballs, and steaming drinks that come with little umbrellas and overflow like gentle volcanoes.

Well, tonight Pip didn't eat much, and I could tell she was trying not to think about the giant seventh-grade boy-girl party that was going on right then.

Dad looked at all the food on our plates, and next thing you know, he started talking about rotten potatoes.

He said that in the middle of the 1800s, almost all the potatoes in Ireland went rotten, and there were "political problems," and a million people starved to death, and another million left the country.

Obviously, this was a terrible tragedy and not "the luck of

the Irish." But if Dad's great-great-grandfather had *not* gotten on a boat to Boston, he would *not* have met my great-great-grandmother, and there'd be *no* Dad, *no* Pip, and *no* **me**.

I would *not* have been born!!

Mom would have been born, but she would have been just a random lady named Anna, not my M-O-M—which is very strange to think about!!

Anyway, we were about to order cake for dessert, but Pip said, "I hate when waiters sing to me." Personally, I *love* when waiters sing to me.

We drove home, and Mom, Dad, and I sang to Pip in our kitchen. She blew out the candles, and we ate some of the gigantic strawberry birthday cake. (Mom had canceled the balloons.)

It was pretty pitiful. Mom tried to liven things up by telling us about a boxer dog who ate his owner's underwear. "His *boxers*?" I asked, and Mom said, "No, it was a pair of pink panties!" I thought that was funny, but Pip looked like she couldn't care less about what kind of undies the dumb dog ate.

Dad tried to liven things up by saying that thirteen is a special number because if you rearrange the letters in "ELEVEN PLUS TWO," you get "TWELVE PLUS ONE." I thought that was funny, but Pip looked like she wasn't in the mood.

At least she got a lot of presents—way more than I ever get!

Mom and Dad gave her a watercolor set and a cell phone, and I gave her *Great Expectations* because the main character's name is Pip. (It was Mr. Ramirez's suggestion.) Unfortunately,

Pip already has that book, so now it's like I haven't given her anything!

A

P.S. Psssst: Pip doesn't need presents anyway. She needs friends— and maybe for her crush, whoever he is, to like her back. Is that asking for a miracle?

10/11
BEDTIME

Dear Diary,

Maybelle came over, and we took turns walking around backward and blindfolded while the other person gave directions on where to go. Then we polished off Pip's strawberry cake—bit by bit and bite by bite.

After Maybelle left, I spent all day writing. Dad said to think BIG, but a bee is small. I wrote the story by hand, then typed it on our computer. I had to check the word count over and over and kept adding and subtracting words as if I were working on a math problem, not a library story. Finally I put a moral at the end, the way Aesop does after his fables. If you include everything from the title to the moral, the story comes to exactly four hundred words.

I'm handing it in tomorrow, on the due date. Dad congratulated me for meeting the "deadline." I said I didn't like that word. *Deadline* makes writing sound dangerous. Which it isn't, 'tis it (T-I-S-I-T)?

I printed out an extra copy and am stapling it here:

Sting of the Queen Bee
by Ava Wren, Age 10

Once upon a time, there was a new girl in school. Her name was Bea. She was mean and she was a thief. She didn't steal erasers or candy or key chains. She didn't steal money or clothes or jewelry. She stole other people's friends.

She did it without even thinking, because she wanted to have as many girls as possible in her group. If someone didn't have many friends of her own, it made Bea extra happy to steal them for her clique, which she called her hive. She didn't care about the girls themselves—she just cared about how many she could get.

In the middle of middle school, Bea had more friends than anyone in seventh grade. But deep down, she felt lonely. She knew she was not a nice person. She knew she was evil, selfish, and rude. And she knew nobody liked her for her. They liked her because her family had a pool and her freezer was full of Popsicles.

One afternoon, Bea and her so-called friends were at her pool when a queen bee—a real queen bee with a teeny tiny crown—was buzzing around looking for flowers. Buzz! Buzz! It landed right on Bea's big nose. The bee stared at Bea; Bea stared at the bee. Then it flew off toward the other girls and listened to their conversations. It was surprised! The girls were whispering and saying that Bea was a friend stealer and a queen bee!

"A queen bee?" the queen bee said to herself. "I'm the only queen bee around here!"

It buzzed straight back to Bea's big nose and stung her twice with its stinger. It wanted to teach Bea a lesson. And it did! Ouch! Ouch!

Bea's nose got red, sore, swollen, and bigger than ever. She put a giant Band-Aid on it and spent two days at home watching TV and feeling very sorry for herself.

Meanwhile, the other girls went back to school, and since Bea wasn't there, they hung out with all the old friends they had dumped—all those loyal girls who'd been kind since kindergarten. Everyone forgave everyone, and everyone got all their friends back.

As for Queen Bea, she learned her lesson: you can't be a friend thief and get away with it.

Moral: There's no shortcut to true friendship.

AVA THE AUTHOR

DEAR DIARY,

I wonder who else in school knows about the contest. No one is buzzing about it. (Get it? Buzzing??)

I keep picturing myself getting good news and telling Mom and Dad, "Now I won!!" (N-O-W-I-W-O-N).

A #1 AVA

DEAR DIARY,

Another 100 on another spelling test.

AVA WHO GETS AS ON FRIDAYS

Dear Diary,

In language arts, Mrs. Lemons said that good writers notice things, and today, while Pip and I carved a jack o' lantern, I noticed that Pip has fewer freckles in the fall than in the summer and that they are lighter now too.

"Wanna play the Homonym Game?" I said. It's when we make sentences with words that sound the same but mean different things, like NUN and NONE, and CHEWS and CHOOSE, and HAIR and HARE. And BEE and BEA and BE.

Pip said, "Not really," but since she didn't say "no," I started. I said, "The FAIRY took a FERRY."

"She had to BURY a BERRY," Pip replied halfheartedly.

"BUT a bee bit her BUTT!"

"They DISCUSSED it with DISGUST," Pip said, then added, "I don't want to play anymore."

"Oh c'mon," I pleaded. "The tennis star hoped to CRUSH her CRUSH!"

Pip squinted at me and said, "I'm not telling you who my crush is, and I'm not playing anymore."

Well, of course that meant I wasn't either.

On the one hand, I feel sorry for Pip. On the other, her bad moods are annoying!

Ava the Annoyed

DEAR DIARY,

I asked Pip to tell me her Homonym Joke.

"Why?"

"Because I want to write it in my diary."

She sighed as if telling me her joke was a big fat favor. Finally she said: "Why is six afraid of seven?"

"Why?"

"Because seven ATE nine."

I jumped around repeating, "Because 7-8-9!" a couple of times, but Pip rolled her eyes. That got me mad, and I ended up shouting, "Why can't you ever just be happy?!"

Of course, that got *her* mad, and she stomped off and shut her door—which made me wish I'd shut my mouth.

AVA THE ANNOYING?

10/19
AFTER SCHOOL

DEAR DIARY,

Lunch was fish sticks. I saw Pip eating alone in the corner, but I sat with my friends.

We talked about the contest. Maybelle didn't enter because she's better with numbers than words. (She just joined Mathletes.) One of the Emilys wrote about zombies, and Mr. Ramirez had to break it to her that zombies are not living creatures. (Duh.) Matthew wrote about a fire-breathing dragon, but dragons are not living creatures either, and besides, he came up with only eighty-three words.

Riley wrote a love story about her pony. All she ever talks about is her pony. Some girls are boy-crazy, but Riley is pony-crazy.

The only other submission I know about in the fourth and fifth grade category is from a dweeby boy named Alex. He wrote about an earthworm named Ernie.

I feel sorry for the judge who has to slog through a story of a BORING worm that goes BORING in the dirt. (Homonym alert!)

At least my story has a beginning, middle, and end, as well as a plot twist. (*Buzz! Buzz!* Ouch! Ouch!)

I told Dad that I wrote about a mean queen bee, and he said that sounded clever. But he smiled in a way that made me wonder if it also sounded dumb.

Should I have given my four hundred words to Dad to fix? Too late now! I also thought of having Mom take a look, but she was always online or busy with Pip. Besides, Mr. Ramirez said we were supposed to write our stories "without any outside help," and that "getting assistance would be inappropriate."

Well, I'm crossing my fingers and hoping to win. If I win, it might be like a small step to becoming a real writer.

AVA THE APPROPRIATE

DEAR DIARY,

Question: Do I even want to be a real writer?

AVA THE AMBIVALENT (WHICH I'M PRETTY *SURE* MEANS *UNSURE*)

10/21
AFTER DINNER

DEAR DIARY,

After school, I went to the vet's, and I got to *pet* some *pet*s. A yellow lab named Butterscotch started wagging his tail the second he saw me. His owner goes away a lot, and Butterscotch always carries a stuffed-animal fox in his mouth. I also pet Panther, a black kitten with a pink nose. He started purring before I even touched him.

Poor pets! They deserve wayyy more attention than they get!!

I liked hanging out with the animals, but I *really* wanted to hang out with Mom. I even said so, but she said, "Ava, shhh. I have piles of files to get through before we have to pick up Pip."

"Fine," I said. But it wasn't fine. Sometimes it seems as if Mom cares more about Pip than about me. Pip, her precious firstborn. Here are three pieces of evidence:

1. Mom always buys Pip her favorite snacks (like pretzels and mangoes), but doesn't buy me mine (like grapes and cheddar cheese).
2. Mom gives Pip an allowance, but I have to take the garbage out for nothing.

3. Mom praises Pip's sketches more than my writing—not that I ever show her my writing, but still.

I didn't even tell Mom that I got another 100 in spelling (or that I got a 79 on a math quiz).

Since I didn't want to accuse Mom of playing favorites, I said, "Sometimes it seems like you care more about animals than about me."

She looked surprised. "What makes you say that?"

"Do you even know what I've been working on?"

"Dad said you entered a writing contest."

"That's right," I said, hoping she'd ask about my story. I was thinking of showing her a copy and telling her that I want to get first prize.

But all she said was: "See? I pay attention." Then she went back to her computer.

Question: *does* Mom like Pip more than me??

Well, at least writing all this down is making me feel a little better. Even though I still miss my magic pen.

AVA THE UNAPPRECIATED

10/23
BEFORE DINNER

Dear Diary,

The phone rang. Our caller ID said, "Misty Oaks Library," so I picked up and said, "Hello."

"Hello. This is Mrs. White at the library. May I please speak to Ava Wren?"

Since she was being formal, I said, "This is she." Pip made a face because "This is she" sounds so dorky.

"I'm calling about the contest. Congratulations! Your story received an honorable mention."

I didn't know what to say. I didn't want to get *mentioned*—honorably or dishonorably. I wanted to win. I wanted to be the ONE who WON!

Mrs. White said my entire family was invited to a 6 p.m. reception on October 28 with "punch and nibbles." She said a famous author, Jerry Valentino, was the judge and would be there.

I was tempted to say, "I've never heard of him, so how famous can he be?" But I thanked her, stuck a note on Dad's computer that said "10/28 6 p.m. Library," and shoved my turquoise pen to the bottom of my backpack.

AVA AND PIP

Obviously, it's *not* a lucky pen, let alone a magic one.

AVA, ABOVE AVERAGE BUT NOT AWARD-WINNING

DEAR DIARY,

I told Dad about the phone call, and he congratulated me. He also said that before Mrs. White got married, her name was Miss Bright, so now her full name is Wendy Bright White. ☺

At dinner, I *mentioned* my honorable *mention* but didn't make a big deal of it because:

1. I didn't come in first.
2. Why bother?
3. When Pip is bummed out, it doesn't feel right to act as happy as a lark.

Mom congratulated me, then said, "I wonder how many submissions they got." Well, that made me wonder if the only reason I even got an honorable mention is that not very many people entered. And that made me upset inside.

Pretty soon we all went back to talking about regular stuff (except Pip who went back to not talking).

I wish Pip felt sunnier. Living with her these days is like living with a rain cloud.

That's a simile.

A simile, according to Mrs. Lemons, is when you describe something using "like" or "as."

If I say, "Pip is quiet as a mouse," that's also a simile, because I'm comparing Pip to a mouse.

I don't think Pip would appreciate any of my similes.

AVA WREN, *NOT* AS HAPPY AS A LARK

Dear Diary,

Maybelle came over with ginger cookies from a batch that she and her mom had baked for a game.

We painted our nails orange and let them dry, and then we wet our fingers and made whistle-y sounds by rubbing them around the tops of our water glasses. We also slid down the stairs on a bath mat. It was fun until I landed on my butt. Owwww! Owwwwch!

I can't complain though because:

1. It's embarrassing to talk about your butt.
2. Mom and Dad might say I'm old enough to know better, or
3. Mom and Dad might not say anything at all.

Here's what worries me: What if I broke my butt? Can butts get broken? Like arms and legs? And hearts?

AVA THE ACHY

10/28
BEDTIME

DEAR DIARY,

Brace yourself because I have a *lot* to tell you. I'll start with the good part, then get to the BAD part.

When Dad and I arrived at the library, Mr. Ramirez asked Dad if he was working on a new play. Dad said, "Yes, but tonight is all about my daughter." He put his arm around me, and it was half-sweet, half-embarrassing.

Soon everyone sat down on folding gray chairs. None of the Emilys were there and neither was Chuck or Matthew (the boy who wrote about dragons). But Riley (pony girl) and Alex (earthworm boy) were. Alex is the kind of boy who burps without saying, "Excuse me," but tonight he was dressed up and on his best behavior. There were kids from other schools too. Everyone was sitting in the room with the high ceilings and high bookcases. Mom and Pip were "on their way."

Mrs. (Bright) White had on a black scarf dotted with pumpkins. She introduced the famous-ish author, Jerry Valentino. He was tall and skinny and looked like he'd forgotten to comb his hair. He said that when he was our age, he loved libraries:

69

"the smell of books, the wooden tables, the peace and quiet." He said his family was "loud and noisy," so as soon as he could, he got a library card. It took him "many years and many rejection letters," but when he was twenty-nine, he published his first children's book.

He lifted it in the air. It was called *Campfire Nights*.

On the cover were three boys and a giant bonfire. I couldn't tell if they were roasting hot dogs or toasting marshmallows, but it was the kind of cover that if you judged a book by its cover, you'd want to buy it. For a second, I pictured myself as a famous-ish author talking to a roomful of kids and lifting a book in the air.

Judge Jerry said there were many "outstanding" submissions and that it had not been easy to choose winners. "We'll start with best story by a fourth- or fifth-grader," he said. Riley and I kept sneaking peeks at each other. I think we each thought the other had come in first.

"This year's winning story," Judge Jerry announced, "is about the underground adventures of an earthworm."

What?! I couldn't believe it! Ernie the Earthworm snagged first prize? Top spot (T-O-P-S-P-O-T)?

"Alex Gladstone's writing is so detailed," Judge Jerry continued, "I could smell the moist dirt! Alex, come tell us what inspired you to set your story deep in the bowels of the earth."

Bowels of the earth? Earth bowels?? Eww!!

Alex stood up. He was wearing a navy jacket and maroon tie and looked even dweebier than usual. Judge Jerry lowered the microphone and Alex breathed into it. I felt almost sorry for him because you could tell that he hadn't expected to have to talk.

After a *lot* of breathing, Alex said, "Whenever I go fishing, I feel bad for the worms, so I wanted to write a worm story with a happy ending." Everyone clapped, and Judge Jerry handed him a certificate and a shiny pen in a velvety box. I was jealous, even though I knew it was pathetic to be jealous of a worm-obsessed fourth-grader.

Judge Jerry raised the microphone and said, "The next two stories were so good that I am honored to award two honorable mentions." He started reading a passage about a pony's "trusting brown eyes," and I wanted to barf because it sounded as if now even Judge Jerry had a crush on Riley's stupid pony.

Riley strutted to the podium as if she were accepting an Academy Award. Her parents were there and so was her sister. Mom and Pip still hadn't arrived, and I kept thinking: "Where are they?"

When Judge Jerry asked Riley what inspired her, she said, "Ponies and horses are my favorite living creatures—besides people."

I thought, "Oh puh-lease!" but everyone clapped, so I fake-clapped.

"The second honorable mention," Judge Jerry continued, "goes to Ava Wren who wrote 'Sting of the Queen Bee.'" My heart was beating really loudly, but no one else seemed to hear. I looked around again for Mom and Pip. Where were they??

"Don't you love that title?" Judge Jerry asked. "It's a *double entendre*, which is French for 'double meaning.'" (I didn't know

71

that.) "I admire Ava's wordplay and vivid imagination," he continued, "as well as her sense of humor and understanding of social dynamics. Furthermore, her depiction of the villain is both whimsical and believable. Or should I say, 'BEE-lievable'?" He laughed at his own wordplay and invited me up. Dad gave my shoulder a little squeeze, and I stood up and walked to the front of the room. I must have been nervous because it seemed like it was a long, long way from my seat to the podium even though obviously it wasn't.

Judge Jerry met my eyes. "Ava, what inspired you?" he said and lowered the microphone.

Well, I couldn't exactly talk about how I'd wanted to get back at the seventh-grade bully who'd ruined my sister's birthday, so I said, "I enjoy observing older kids," and hoped I didn't sound like a spy.

"Wonderful!" Judge Jerry said. "Keen observation is an important tool in every writer's toolbox."

Everyone clapped, and for a second, I thought I spotted Mom in the back of the room. But I was wrong. She really had missed my big moment.

I sat back down next to Dad feeling one-third proud, one-third mad at Mom and Pip, and one-third worried about them, when the library door creaked open.

In walked not Mom, not Pip, but…Bea! Queen Bea!! With her family!!!

Bea was the *last* person I expected to see! Really! I was Ava the Astonished! And she arrived just seconds after Judge Jerry had exclaimed over my "BEE-lievable" villain!

I'd assumed that writing wasn't dangerous, but was I wrong? Dead wrong?

What if Bea finds out what I wrote? And why, oh why didn't I think of that earlier??

I'd tell you what happened next, but my hand is about to fall off. (Figuratively, not literally.)

To be continued…

AVA THE AFRAID

10/29
BEFORE SCHOOL

DEAR DIARY,

So here's what happened: when Bea walked into the library, I tried not to look nervous, scared, or petrified. She saw me and smiled as if she recognized me from our middle school. I did *not* smile back!

Well, the first prize in the sixth- and seventh-grade category went to a boy from an all-boys' school. His story was about a *penguin* with a *pen*, and Judge Jerry said it illustrated "the extraordinary power of words." The boy stepped up but did not say a single solitary word, let alone any extraordinary powerful ones. He just got redder and redder (R-E-D-D-E-R and R-E-D-D-E-R) until he sat down again.

"The next honorable mention," Judge Jerry announced, "goes to seventh-grader Beatrice Bates who wrote a story called 'Bookshop Cat.' Bea, come on up!" She hopped up, and he welcomed her on stage and asked what inspired her.

She flicked her long blond hair behind her ears and leaned into the microphone and said, "I'm a cat person, and my parents are book people. They own a bookshop."

I looked at Dad, and he was smiling. Clearly he had *not* put two and two together. Why would he? Nobody realized that the villain in my story was standing in front of our very eyes, basking in the library limelight. I couldn't believe Bea-Bee the two-faced was attempting to come off as a decent person! What a little faker! Everyone (except me) clapped until she sat down, all full of herself.

If only people knew what she was really like!!

Judge Jerry gave the last honorable mention to an eighth-grader named Charona who has lavender braces and wrote "a humorous story" about a timid turtle named Timmy who wouldn't come out of his shell. Charona was there with her parents, grandparents, and even a teacher.

Finally it was time for "punch and nibbles." A photographer told us "winners" to smoosh together and say, "Stories!" with a big cheesy "eeeeez" at the end. Guess who plunked herself right next to me and started smiling away? Bea! I fake-smiled as well as I could.

Outside, I may have looked happy, but inside, I was worried. If Bea found out about my story, would she punch or nibble *me*? Bea bruises and Bea bites were something I did not want!!

Mrs. (Bright) White tapped the microphone and said, "Thank you all for coming, and don't forget to pick up your free copies of this year's *Winning Words*." She pointed to a big stack of sky-blue booklets, which were really just colored paper that got printed on and folded over and stapled in the middle. I started praying that the booklets included only the stories that won-won, *not* the stories that got mentioned-mentioned.

"Every story is in here," Mrs. (Bright) White continued, "so you're in for a treat. Congratulations again to all our winners and their proud families."

My heart sank to my belly button. A *treat*? If Bea read my story, I'd be dead *meat*!

I looked over at Bea. She was talking with her parents and brother. He's in eighth grade and has sandy hair and is new in school too (duh). He has as many freckles as Pip and is the kind of boy who's cute if you're the kind of girl who notices. Which I'm not.

Riley's mom asked if she could take a picture for us, and Dad handed her his camera. But it was APPARENT that I was with just A PARENT. Where *were* Mom and Pip?

I get that Pip's favorite place is home-sweet-home (which she's turning into home-sour-home). But they'd told me they were coming!

Riley's mom took pictures anyway, and I tried my best to real-smile, not fake-smile.

Soon I started wondering if we were all taking this contest too seriously. Judge Jerry was making it sound like we were destined to be the next J. K. Rowlings or Judy Blumes, but c'mon, we're just a bunch of kids writing about worms and ponies and bees. Were we like those sports teams where everyone gets a shiny trophy, even if she can't catch a fly ball to save her life?

When Dad and I finally got back to our sweet-and-sour home, Pip and Mom were there. Pip said she'd gotten stomach cramps at the last minute, and Mom said she hadn't wanted to leave her alone. I didn't ask Pip whether it was because of her "stage of life" or her allergy to people. I was just sorry she'd missed the reception and mad that because of her, Mom had too.

Now I'm wondering if, deep down, Mom was a tiny bit relieved that her favorite daughter wouldn't have to listen to a bunch of people clapping for her *other* daughter. Or maybe Mom thought Pip had something serious—like appendicitis? Or that going to the reception didn't matter much because it was just a dumb kid contest, and Dad showed up and besides, I didn't really win?

Secret: it *did* matter!!!

Here's my new worry: What will happen when Bea reads my story? Will *Bea bea*t me up? Or turn all of Misty Oaks Middle School against me? I wish I'd never entered the stupid contest!

I wish my writer's block had blocked me for real!

AVA IN AGONY

DEAR DIARY,

No Bea stings in school. No Bea bites either. Maybe Bea threw away her *Winning Words*, and my little story won't get me in big trouble?

As for my library booklet, I was going to put it on Mom and Dad's bed, but I didn't want to get disappointed if they didn't like it—or didn't read it.

Besides, since Dad saw Bea on stage, what if he figured things out and instead of being proud of me, started asking questions?

I decided to stash the booklet under my underwear in my dead diary graveyard.

Then I changed my mind again and put it in Pip's room by a sketchpad with a note that said: "For Your Eyes Only, see page 8." I'd meant to show it to her when I first wrote it.

Speaking of Pip, she's hardly *speaking*. She brought a book to dinner, but Mom made her put it away.

I wish Pip weren't so moody, or should I say, bad-moody?

I also wish I didn't care. But when she gets down, it gets me down. Her moods are contagious—I'm like a sponge for bad feelings.

AVA THE SPONGE

10/30
AFTER SCHOOL

DEAR DIARY,

Bea passed me in the hall today smiling as though we're besties. I half-smiled back because I didn't know what else to do.

Does this mean I can relax? Because when I see Bea, I still feel very jjUUmmPPyy.

It's insane! At school, I worry about Bea, and at home, I worry about Pip!

Tomorrow is Halloween. Maybelle came over, and we played Hangman. I won with "gypsy" because Maybelle wasted five guesses on the regular vowels, A-E-I-O-U.

Afterward, we microwaved marshmallows. At first, it got messy because we nuked them too long. Then we got the hang of it, and we even invented variations like adding jelly beans and chocolate chips.

We also planned our Halloween costumes: we are going as yellow-and-black-striped bumblebees. (*Not* queen bees!)

Tomorrow I am not going to think about anything except candy. Candy. Candy. Candy. Candy. Candy.

Sweet!

AVA WITH AN APPETITE

DEAR DIARY,

Halloween can also be spelled Hallowe'en because the *e'en* stands for "evening." Dad said it's from All Hallows' Eve—which is the night before All Saints' Day, which is when ghosties go floating around. (Not really.)

Pip is staying home tonight to help Mom give out candy.

I invited Pip to trick-or-treat with me and Maybelle. Mom didn't even have to ask. But I didn't beg her or anything. If Pip wants to be antisocial, that's her problem, not mine. I mean, it's not my fault that she's not *outgoing* and doesn't like *going out*.

Observation: all year long, parents say, "Don't eat too much candy," but on October 31, no one cares.

Here's my two cents on that:

1. Y-A-Y
2. M-M-M

AVA IN COSTUME

11/1
1:11

DEAR DIARY,

Today's date and time would be a number palindrome (111111) if you left out the dash and dots, which no one does, so never mind.

I reread what I wrote yesterday: "If Pip wants to be antisocial, that's her problem, not mine." But that's not totally true, is it? When one family member is sick or stressed or writer's-blocky, it affects everybody. Or *infects* everybody.

Like right now, I feel like saying, "Hey, Pip, did you read my story?" or "Hey, Pip, want to watch a movie?" But she'd just say something gloomy, so I'm being as quiet as she is. We're like *two* mice!

I feel bad for Pip, but I also feel like yelling at her again!!

Last night after trick-or-treating, I was going to show her my bag of candy, including some palindromic Milk D-U-Ds and Blow P-O-Ps, but I didn't want to make her feel worse about missing a fun night. Later, Mom went in, and they talked for a long, long time. That made me mad, because I'd set aside five red licorice sticks—Mom's favorite—but I fell asleep before she came to say good night.

Things are too quiet around here. Personally, I don't like living in the House of Silence. We're the Wrens! We're supposed to be singing!

AVA WREN, SONGBIRD

11/1
SUNDAY NIGHT

DEAR DIARY,

Dad gave us snack money, so Pip and I biked to Taco Time, which is four blocks away. We rode past the yellow, orange, and red trees, and I tried to remember the last time we even went. We used to go every week!

The first time was last spring. Dad was tutoring a high school junior, and Pip and I were starving, so he handed us $14 and said, "Take care of each other." And off we went—all by ourselves.

Today when our tacos came, I saw a Toyota out the window, so I said, "A Toyota!" (A-T-O-Y-O-T-A). Pip was supposed to reply, "A Toyota's a Toyota!" (A-T-O-Y-O-T-A-S-A-T-O-Y-O-T-A), which is our family's new inside joke. But she didn't.

"You okay?" I asked.

"Why wouldn't I be?" she said. And I realized that the person I really wanted to yell at is Queen Bea. Just thinking about that girl drives me 100 percent *crazy*!

Pip must have read my mind, because she said, "Hey, Ava, I meant to tell you, I liked your story."

"Really?" I tried to sound casual.

"Yes. It was funny. And I know you meant well." I waited for her to say more about my way with words or how she was glad I'd trashed her archenemy. "But I wonder what Bea Bates is going to think," she continued. "She might freak out. She *is* a real person, after all."

Well, that made me so nervous, I forgot to hold my taco properly, and the beef and sour cream insides came sliding out and plopped onto the table and some splattered onto my lap.

Did I really pick a fight with a popular seventh-grader? How could I be so dumb?

"Maybe she won't read it?" I said. "At school, she always smiles at me."

Pip shrugged.

AVA THE DOOMED

DEAR DIARY,

I passed Bea in the hall this morning, and she did *not* smile at me. She gave me an odd look.

I spent the rest of the day trying not to panic.

In language arts, I finally got a little distracted because Mrs. Lemons was talking about "perspective" (which she said is like "point of view") and was going over spelling words (including the bonus word "throughway"). She said there are many ways to pronounce "ough," and on the board, she wrote:

1. "oo" as in thr*ough*
2. "oh" as in th*ough*
3. "uff" as in en*ough*
4. "off" as in *cough*
5. "aw" as in *ough*t and
6. "ow" as in b*ough*

I said, "That's so cool!" at the same exact time that Chuck said, "That's so complicated!" Everyone laughed. Even Mrs. Lemons.

At home, I wanted to tell Dad about the "ough" thing, but he and Pip just went out to buy groceries.

Probably pretzels and mangoes.

EY•VUH

DEAR DIARY,

The phone rang, and instead of checking caller ID, I picked up like an idiot. I thought it would be Dad, and I was going to ask him to buy some grapes.

"Hello," I said.

"Is this Ava?"

"Yes…" My heart started doing flip-flops because I thought I recognized the voice.

"It's Bea. Bea Bates."

I didn't know whether to hang up, apologize, defend myself, or say, "Wrong number."

"Hi," I mumbled.

"Hi," she repeated. Why had I picked up? Pip never picks up! She lets the machine take messages unless it's Dad or Mom or me.

"First of all," Bea began, "I don't have a big nose."

I was torn between saying, "I don't know what you're talking about" and "Poetic license." Dad says writers get a "poetic license" when they exaggerate to make a point.

"Second, I don't have a pool or a lifetime supply of Popsicles."

I kept quiet.

"And third, I am not rude, but your story was."

"Rude?" I repeated, which meant that so far, all I'd said was: "Yes," "Hi," and "Rude?" I'd heard of one-liners, but never one-worders. Bea was making me as tongue-tied as Pip!

"Why did you write about me like that?" she asked.

"My story isn't about you! It's about a girl with a big nose and a big pool…" Suddenly I was glad no one was home, because I didn't want Dad or Mom or Pip to hear me trying to defend my story.

"Named Bea? Who's new? Ava, don't insult my intelligence."

I went quiet again. I didn't want to insult her intelligence, but I didn't want her to insult me either.

"You know what? Maybe you're right," Bea continued. "Your story is *not* about me. But you should think twice before you set out to ruin someone's reputation."

"Well, *you* should think twice before you set out to ruin someone's birthday!" I blurted, surprising myself. "My sister still hasn't gotten over it!"

"Excuse me? How was I supposed to know your sister was having a party that day?" Bea asked. "I barely knew she existed! If she or her friends had said something, I could've invited her. No big deal. So blame Pip, not me."

"Wait. You're saying it's *Pip's* fault you stole her friends?!"

"Stole her friends?! Ava, you're in fifth grade, right? When you're my age, you'll realize that friends aren't objects you can steal. I'm friendly, so I have lots of friends. Your sister is unfriendly, so she doesn't. To be honest, when I first met Pip, I thought she was a snob because she keeps to herself so much."

What?! Did Pip really come off as a *snob*? Do some people think she doesn't talk because she thinks she's too good for them? "You shouldn't say mean things about someone you don't know!" I said and started pacing around our living room with the phone at my ear.

"You shouldn't *write* mean things about someone you don't know!" she shot back. "And I'm *not* a queen bee. *You* are a drama queen!"

"Me?"

"You! What was my big crime anyway? Throwing a party? Because *yours* was jumping to conclusions and writing a malicious story."

I stopped pacing and quickly looked up "malicious" on Dad's computer.

The dictionary said "intending to do harm."

Whoa. Had I *intended* to do harm? I felt dizzy. My Queen Bee story was supposed to be about kindness, but was the story itself *unkind*? Was *I*? I was starting to feel like a rotten potato.

"Ava? Are you still there?"

"Yes," I said, and mumbled "I'm sorry" into the phone.

"Sorry you wrote what you wrote, or sorry I found out?"

"Both," I replied before realizing that was *not* the best answer.

"Well, you *should* be! How would you feel if I wrote a story about a mean fifth-grader named Ava?"

"Bad."

"Exactly. And for your information, when you write something down, it doesn't go away. It's not like talking on the phone."

I nodded, but since we *were* talking on the phone, I forced myself to say, "Okay."

"But don't you see? That's my point: it's *not* okay. From now on, whoever reads your story at school will think less of *me* or less of *you*." I hadn't thought of it that way and slumped into Dad's chair. "For the record," she continued, "I had to read your story three times just to be sure I wasn't being paranoid."

I pictured Bea reading 400 x 3 = 1,200 of my words. If it had been a regular story, I would have felt incredibly proud. Instead I felt like a potato with mold all over it.

How many other copies of *Winning Words* were out there for me to worry about. Forty? Fifty?

I went upstairs and into Pip's messy room, holding the phone to my ear. The sky-blue booklet was on her desk, and I picked it up.

"I finally asked Isabel about it," Bea was saying, "and she explained everything. I just wish she'd said something then! Or that your sister had! I gave that party to make friends, not enemies."

I carried *Winning Words* into my room and stuck it in my dead diary graveyard where it could keep my underwear and my Loser Words company.

"Ava, are you even there?"

I said, "Yes," but didn't know what else to say because I was starting to see things from Bea's side. I was about to mumble "Sorry" again when she said, "My aunt said I should call you, so

I did. But that's it. We're done. I just wanted to give you a piece of my mind."

I pictured myself holding a piece of Bea's mind, which was a pretty disgusting image, to tell you the truth.

Bea hung up and I did too. But I wished I'd apologized better.

I also wish I *weren't* alone in the house anymore, because right now I'm feeling alone in the world.

AVA, ALONE AND APOLOGETIC

Dear Diary,

Dad and I were sitting on the sofa. He picked up his big fat thousand-page book. "What if James Joyce had written about two days instead of one day?" I asked. "Would *Ulysses* have been two thousand pages long?"

He laughed and said he wanted to read *my* story. I said I misplaced it. He said, "Really?" like he didn't quite believe me. I said, "Really" because it was sort of true: I'd *placed* it where it would be *miss*ing!

To be honest, I don't like being less than honest with Dad. I mean, I wish I could just tell him everything and have him hug me and tell me it's all going to be okay.

But what if he got disappointed in me instead? Or thought everything was *not* going to be okay? I don't think I could take it.

Anyway, Dad went back to reading, and I wrote Bea an apology note in my very best handwriting.

I'm going to deliver it tomorrow before homeroom.

Here's what it says:

AVA AND PIP

DEAR BEA,

I REALLY AM SORRY. I WAS JUST TRYING TO HELP MY SISTER.

AVA

It's late, and I hope I can fall asleep.

ASININE AVA

P.S. I *swear* "asinine" is not a *swear* word. It means really foolish and idiotic.

DEAR DIARY,

I slept terribly. I dreamed a vicious bee with a tiny tiara was buzzing around my head and would not buzz off.

At breakfast, I was exhausted. Dad opened the fridge and said, "No melon, no lemon" (N-O-M-E-L-O-N, N-O-L-E-M-O-N). Then he said, "Aha!" (A-H-A) and picked up a shriveled olive. "An evil olive!" (E-V-I-L-O-L-I-V-E). Then he bit into a banana.

Mom said, "Yo, Banana Boy!" (Y-O-B-A-N-A-N-A-B-O-Y). "It's too early. Besides, I have a headache. And I already took one lonely Tylenol" (L-O-N-E-L-Y-T-Y-L-E-N-O-L).

Pip and I looked at each other, and I thought: no wonder Pip doesn't talk much in public. When it comes to conversation, our parents are very peculiar role models.

I told my family I had a nightmare, but didn't say it was a night*bee*.

"I'm sorry," Dad said, then added, "I guess I'd better not tell you girls about what I'm working on."

"Why not?" Pip asked.

"Because it would give you both bad dreams!"

"Tell us!" Pip and I said, right on cue. Then we both said, "Jinx!"

Dad smiled and said, "You know how there are lots of books about vampires?"

"Yes," Pip said.

"Well, the first good one was *Dracula*, and I'm trying to turn it into a play for kids. It was by an Irish writer."

Mom leaned her head on her hand in a tired way, while Dad explained that the author, Bram Stoker, got the idea from a church in Dublin. The church was so dry and cool inside that the bodies in its crypt barely decomposed. They looked alive even though they were dead!

For a second, I pictured Little Bram Stoker as a ten-year-old in a navy jacket and maroon tie telling a contest audience how inspiring it was to observe a bunch of non-rotting corpses.

Mom looked up. "Really, Bob? You're telling our daughters about corpses first thing in the morning?"

Dad shrugged, but the funny thing is, I didn't mind hearing about the creepy, well-preserved corpses because it gave me "per-spective." I mean, at least I'm—

AVA, AWAKE AND ALIVE

11/3
AFTER SCHOOL, IN THE LIBRARY

DEAR DIARY,

Before homeroom, I walked down the school hall and up to Bea's locker, which I'd noticed was close to Pip's. I looked both ways, slipped my note in, and ran. Instead of my phone number, which she obviously had, I wrote my locker number next to my name.

An hour later, I noticed a corner of a yellow piece of paper sticking out of my locker. I could feel every one of my nerves jingling, but I reached for the note and opened it up. The handwriting was bad, but I deciphered it and here it is:

> Ava,
>
> Meet me at my Locker after Seventh period
>
> bea

I was tempted to write her a note back saying I had a dentist appointment, and I thought: How am I going to survive until seventh period?

Well, you know how time can go fast or slow? Today *time* took its *time*! All the minute hands on the wall clocks seemed stuck, and I kept trying to figure out what I should say to Bea.

When the bell finally rang after seventh period, I went to her locker. I stood there like an idiot and watched the entire school rush by, nice kids and mean kids, nice teachers and scary teachers, and even Principal Gupta, who is strict, and Nurse Abrahams, who is sweet. (I wanted to call out, "Nurse Abrahams! Help! Help! S-O-S! S-O-S!")

It was almost time for math when Bea showed up. "Have you thought about what you did?" she asked.

"Yes." She looked at me, waiting for more. "I was trying to help my sister, but what I wrote wasn't fair, and I'm sorry. I apologize again."

She stared at me for a while then said, "You should have left me out of it. And there are better ways to help your sister. Tell you what, Ava, why don't you meet me after school in the library?"

Another meeting? I didn't want another meeting!

The bell rang, and I mumbled, "Okay," and ran to math. I didn't want to be late because Mrs. Hamshire gets mad when kids are late. And she's scary even when she's not mad.

After math, I called Dad and said I was going to the library after school and would get home a little late.

Dad loves libraries, probably even more than Mrs. (Bright) White + Jerry Valentino + Mr. Ramirez combined. So he didn't say, "The library? I forbid it!" He said, "Okay."

So I didn't say, "Dad, if I never make it home, I love you, and blame Bea Bates!" I just said "Okay" back.

Well, it's now 3:05, and I'm in the school library, and Bea is nowhere in sight, and I feel like an inchworm. (That's a sad simile.)

Outside, the branches are blowing every which way. Inside, it feels hot and stuffy.

I'm waiting and waiting and trying to stay calm. The custodian is emptying the waste paper baskets and scraping gum off from under the desks.

Did Bea tell me to stick around just to torture me? Did she mean *today*?

I got out my pleasure-reading book but kept rereading and *rereading* the same page, and it was *not* a pleasure. I took out my spelling notebook and tried to study bonus words, but I couldn't keep my mind on them.

One was "libel," which means writing something "unfavorable" about a person. Well, I now realize that if you LIBEL someone, you're LIABLE to get into big trouble.

Questions:

1. Are my days numbered? My hours? My minutes?
2. Where is Bea??
3. What does she want with me anyway???

AVA IN ANGUISH

11/3
BEDTIME

DEAR DIARY,

At 3:10, Bea came racing in. Mr. Ramirez looked surprised to see Bea (a seventh-grader) heading straight toward me (a fifth-grader).

Suddenly Bea was looming over me all out of breath with a yellow pad and pointy pencil.

"Are you going to write a mean story about me?" I asked. The words came tumbling out.

"What are you talking about?" Bea sat down. "I'm not here for revenge. I'm here to help you help your sister."

"I don't get it," I said. If I were Bea, I'd hold a grudge for a year. Or for life.

"Ava, I've been thinking. You did a bad thing for a good reason. And it does stink about Pip's party. But it's not too late to make things better for her." She pulled a scrunchie off her wrist and put her blond hair into a ponytail. "She can't go through middle school not talking, right? Being painfully shy must be painful."

I was about to defend Pip, but I realized that Bea wasn't attacking her. So I sat there speechless, which is way more Pip-y than Ava-y. Finally I said, "I still don't get it."

"This may sound weird," Bea began, "but when I grow up, I want to be an advice columnist."

"For real?"

"For real. Whenever I pick up a magazine, I turn to the advice column first."

I wasn't sure what to say. I'm not used to seventh-graders confiding in me about their life goals. And not one kid in homeroom had said, "Advice columnist."

"My aunt says I have a lot of common sense, and that that's very *uncommon*," Bea continued. "So look, you want to help Pip, and I want to help people, so maybe we can figure something out."

"Maybe…" I said.

"My big brother used to be really shy, and I helped him. I mean, he's still a little shy, but not as shy as he used to be."

"Huh," I said, remembering the sandy-haired freckled boy at Misty Oaks Library.

"Last summer at camp," she said, "I made a lot of friends on the first day, but it took him weeks to get to know people. He said I was 'the opposite of shy' and asked how I did it. Well, that got me thinking."

"Oh," I said. Bea had turned me back into a one-word wonder.

She met my eyes and said, "Tell me about Pip." I didn't know if I should or not, but Bea had just told me about her brother, so next thing you know, I heard myself telling her that Pip likes big books and small animals and that she's artistic and smart and pretty, but "too quiet for her own good."

Bea said, "Let me sleep on this and let's meet tomorrow. Same table, fifteen minutes before school starts."

I couldn't believe we were scheduling another meeting. It was like we were grown-ups or something.

Now I'm in bed. I told Mom and Dad to wake me early because I had to work on a language arts project. They didn't question that, and it wasn't a total lie anyway because Bea and I want to try to help Pip use the English language.

Funny how some parents ask about every detail of their kids' lives, and some don't.

Question: Mom and Dad *over*protect Pip, but do they *under-*protect me?

AVA ALL ANTSY

Dear Diary,

I got to the library on time, and Bea got there a few minutes late. "You have really good handwriting, right?"

"Right." I almost told her that my favorite letter in cursive is a capital Q because of how it looks a little like a fancy 2: *2*. I did *not* almost tell her that when I was little and my family needed me to be quiet, they'd sometimes give me a page of Os that I would turn into Qs (regular Qs, not cursive *2*s), and that this was my idea of a good time.

"My handwriting's terrible," Bea said, and luckily I did not blurt, "I know" or "I noticed" or "You can say that again." "Tell you what," she continued. "I'll talk, and you write."

"Okay." I dug out my turquoise pen, and Bea handed me a piece of yellow lined paper. She also got out a small spiral notebook that looked pretty worn, and then she started dictating. Well, I was concentrating so hard on spelling and neatness that I hardly even noticed what I was writing. I wanted all the dots on my *i*'s to match, and I didn't want them to be bubbles, hearts, or daisies because I wanted Bea to think I was mature.

When I got to the last word of her "four pointers," she took the paper back.

"Perfect!" she said. She borrowed Mr. Ramirez's scissors and cut the paper into four strips. It felt like we were doing an arts and crafts project.

"Here's the first assignment," Bea said as she handed me a yellow strip. The handwriting was mine, but the words surprised me:

WEEK ONE:
SMILE AT ONE NEW PERSON EVERY DAY.

"If all goes well," Bea stated, "in just one month, we can get your sister to go from a Before to an After."

"Really?" I said and tried to picture Old Pip turning into New-and-Improved Pip. I couldn't see it. "It might take at least five weeks," I said and looked over the strips. "Mind if I add a fifth pointer?"

"Not at all," she said. "I made these up last night, though I guess I have been thinking about them for a while."

I wrote out, "Week Five: Ask someone a question each day. Listen to the answer," because I like when people ask me friendly questions.

"Good one!" Bea said, which made me feel good. She even scribbled it down in her own little notebook.

"Are you going to tell Pip that you want to be an advice columnist and she's your first guinea pig?"

"*Second*," Bea corrected. "Ben was the first, remember? But he wasn't a guinea pig, and neither is Pip. They're more like the timid turtle in that contest story, the one who wouldn't stick his head out."

"Timmy," I said, though I wished she hadn't mentioned the contest.

"Right!" Bea said. "And, Ava, we're not doing this for my *future*. We're doing it for Pip's *present*."

"That's a homonym," I said, then wanted to kick myself. Since it was too late, I kept talking. "PRESENT like 'now' and PRESENT like 'gift.'"

I hoped Bea wouldn't think this was a strange thing to say. It *was* a strange thing to say.

Questions:

1. Why, oh why does my brain work this way?
2. Can I blame B-O-B and A-N-N-A?

Speaking of palindromes, Bea said she liked my name. Since I did *not* want to be speaking of palindromes, I just said, "Thanks."

She said there was a book in her family's store about an actress named Ava Gardner. "That Ava had three husbands, all famous. Frank Sinatra, a singer, Mickey Rooney, an actor, and Artie Shaw, a musician."

"So she wasn't at all shy," I said.

Bea laughed. "What were you reading when I came in?" She reached across and flipped over my book.

"*The Witches*," I said.

"I love Roald Dahl!"

"Me too."

Funny how I'd assumed Bea was a witch and she'd assumed Pip was a snob. I guess people can't help but judge books by their covers and people by their looks.

At school, kids get made fun of if they're dweeby or fat or funny-looking. But even when a girl is cute, like Bea or Pip, some people still think bad things.

I started feeling a little guilty for having assumed that Bea was a jerk and for thinking not-nice thoughts about Alex Gladstone just because he's dweeby and burps out loud.

"Does your bookshop really have a cat?" I asked, because I didn't want to dwell on my shallowness.

"Yes. His name is Meow Meow. He's orange with stripes. He wanders around with his tail in the air, and he knows which customers are cat people and which aren't."

I told her about some of the cats Dr. Gross takes care of, like Fuzz Ball with the three legs and purry Panther with the pink nose. I didn't tell her about Whiskers, since he's dead. And I didn't tell her that Dr. Gross was a grump.

"Does he ever take care of monkeys?" Bea asked, sort of randomly.

"No monkeys, no goldfish," I said. "But he once removed a tumor from a mouse named Stuart Little."

Bea laughed again. "Okay, here's the plan: I'll stop by your house at 4. All you have to do is make sure your sister's alone. Agreed?"

"Agreed," I said, because Pip's always alone.

AVA THE AGREEABLE

DEAR DIARY,

At 4, Pip and I were in the living room. I was having big problems doing decimals, and she was having no problems doing fractions. I casually said, "Bea's coming over."

"Bea?" Pip said. "Did you say *Bea*?"

"Remember 'Sting of the Queen Bee'?"

"Uh, *yeah*."

"Well, Bea thought it was mean that I thought she was mean."

"Wait, wait, wait! You *talked* to her? To Bea Bates?"

I told Pip that Bea called and said she hadn't known Pip was having a party.

Pip stared at me, and I wondered if I'd been a total traitor.

"And you believed that little phony?" Pip said.

"I did. I do." I looked at her. "I know I called her a thief, but now I think she's the opposite. She's a very giving person."

"Oh, Ava! *You're* a very gullible person!" Pip threw her book down and started stomping around the room.

Since Aesop says honesty is the best policy, I told Pip the truth.

"Bea said she helped her brother 'come out of his shell' and now she wants to try her method on you."

"Are you kidding?! I don't need her help! Or her *method*!" Pip said "method" as if she were saying "poison" or "booger" or "throw up." I didn't say anything, and Pip said, "Seriously, Ava, thanks a lot! I bet she's just looking for a new way to humiliate me!"

"I don't think so."

"What's she planning to do anyway? Sprinkle me with popularity powder?" I could tell that Pip was mad, but also a tiny bit curious.

"She isn't planning to *do* anything. She has tips for *you* to do. Pointers." I didn't mention all our meetings or our five-week master plan.

"Thanks, but no thanks. I do not need a personality transplant."

I wanted to shout, "Yes, you do!" But I just sat there and didn't say another word.

At 4:05, I started wondering if Bea was even coming. "Where's Dad, anyway?" I asked.

"Upstairs, putting new wallpaper in the bathroom. He said he had to repaper it and then he looked all happy, because, you know, R-E-P-A-P-E-R. You know what? I'm going to go help him." She started walking upstairs.

"No! Stay here!" I said. "I'll give you M&M's." I still had some from Halloween.

Pip hesitated. She can never resist M&M's. Especially green ones and Minis.

The doorbell rang.

Pip stood frozen in place like a statue. It rang again. I waited. Pip waited. It rang one more time. "Well," Pip finally said, "aren't you planning on opening the door for Bossy Bea, your new best friend?"

I did, and Bea burst in holding a bike helmet. "Hi!" *Bea* was *bea*ming. "How's it going?" she said, walking right in. "Pip, I hope Ava told you I'm sorry about your birthday. I had no clue we were both giving a party on the same day."

Pip didn't say anything, but since she usually doesn't, I couldn't tell what she was thinking.

"Want some gum?" Bea said and offered us some pieces.

"What flavor?" I asked.

"Lemon lime," she said. I took a piece, but Pip didn't.

"Pip," Bea began, "Ava says you're a good student and good artist, but that you're a little shy."

Pip glared at me, and I basically died.

"I was thinking," Bea continued, "that you should take another look at the other kids at school. They're not Olympic athletes or famous musicians or anything. Most are just regular." Now Bea turned to me. "So that's why Ava and I think you could put yourself out there a little more."

When Bea said my name again, I could feel Pip's eyes burning a hole in my head. I wondered if she felt as if we were all playing Battleship, and Bea and I had found her hiding place and were ganging up on her with torpedoes.

I didn't want to upset her, and I felt bad that she was being even more speechless than usual, if that's possible.

Finally Pip started talking. "Listen, Bea, thanks for the apology but—"

"My brother used to be shy," Bea jumped in. "Pip, I think I can help you too. Just give it a try?"

Pip looked cornered. She had obviously not been expecting this pep (P-E-P) talk. Should I have prepared her? Warned her?

"Give *what* a try?" she said.

"Your first assignment."

Pip frowned. "I have enough homework."

"C'mon. Just let me explain?"

Pip shrugged, but it was obvious that she was listening.

"Okay, every day this week," Bea began, "all you have to do is smile at one person you don't usually smile at. It can be a teacher. Or a cashier. Or someone's mom or dad."

Pip didn't say anything, so Bea kept going.

"It can be someone next to you in line, or someone you'll never see again. Or even someone who looks like he or she could use a smile. I'll stop by next week, and you can tell me how it went."

"That's it?" Pip said.

"That's it."

"Just smile?"

"Well, you could try to make a little eye contact too."

Pip looked at me, and our eyes made a little contact. Hers were saying, "Ava, I might have to chop you up into tiny pieces."

"You don't have to be someone you're not," Bea reassured Pip. "Just seven little smiles is all we're asking."

She handed Pip the strip of paper. Pip looked at it suspiciously, as if it really had been dipped in poison or boogers or throw up. I knew she recognized the handwriting—and besides, the turquoise was a dead giveaway. I hoped Pip wouldn't be too mad that I'd opened our home to a girl whose guts, one month ago, we'd both decided we hated.

"Mind if I get a glass of water?" Bea asked. We went to the kitchen, and she got herself a glass. "Thanks," she said and put it in the sink. "I'll be back in a week."

After she left, Pip said, "Who does she think she is, anyway?"

"I don't know," I said, hoping Pip felt at least a teensy bit flattered. It wasn't every day that a popular seventh-grader dropped by.

AVA WITH HOPE

DEAR DIARY,

Pip didn't say anything about Bea's visit, so I didn't either. Not to her or anyone.

After dinner, I put a small pile of green M&M's on Pip's desk. I'd been saving them up. I also wrote her a joke:

> Question: Why did the worker at the M&M factory get fired?
>
> Answer: Because he kept throwing out the Ws.

She didn't say anything about the M&M's or the joke, and since I was bored, I decided to clean my room. I was still looking for my missing pen.

Well, I kept putting things away and did not find the pen. But at least I found the top of my desk!

AVA WITH ABUNDANT M&M'S

11/7
Saturday around noon (N-O-O-N)

Dear Diary,

"Abundant" was one of the bonus words on yesterday's spelling test. After the test, we had to switch papers with the kid next to us and grade each other's. Chuck got a 65. He said spelling doesn't matter because of spell-check. I said that wasn't true, because spell-check can't always help you (and I wrote this part down) "fined yore miss steaks." He studied my words and smiled.

For homework this weekend, Mrs. Lemons gave us an assignment to write about something we read and say what we learned from it. I thought about my lost magic pen and the moral, "No use crying over spilt milk," and I asked if I could write about an Aesop's fable. She said sure.

But which one?

"The Milkmaid and Her Pail"? Naa. Meh. Nuh-uh. (Is that how you spell those words?)

"The Ant and the Grasshopper"? Maybe. I could write about how people (not just ants and grasshoppers) should plan ahead.

"The Tortoise and the Hare"? Maybe. I could write about

how people (not just turtles and bunnies) should strive to reach their goals.

I started thinking that I'm *not* good at planning ahead and setting goals. Then I realized that it was okay because I'm only in fifth grade. And then I watched an origami video and started folding paper flowers.

AVA, AESOP FAN

DEAR DIARY,

After reading (and rereading) a bunch of fables, I decided to write about "The North Wind and the Sun." It's about a bet between the wind and the sun on who can make a traveler take off his coat first. The wind blows and blows as hard as it can, but the more it blows, the more tightly the traveler holds on to his coat. Then the sun takes a turn, and instead of using all its might, it just shines and shines warmly and normally. Next thing you know, the traveler removes his coat. The moral? "Kindness wins where force fails."

Here's what I think: when I wrote that Queen Bee story, I thought I was being *kind*, but I was really being *blind*.

Here's what else I think: you can't force people to change, but you can help them try. Like, Bea and I aren't *forcing* Pip out of her shell, but if she does the assignments, maybe she'll inch out on her own, step by step.

Speaking of Pip, this morning I saw her smile! Our postman rang the doorbell and handed her a bunch of letters. Instead of just taking them silently, she smiled and even said, "Thank you."

The postman's eyes got big, and he said, "You're welcome." Then he shot *me* a look that said, "I didn't know your sister could talk."

That may not sound like much to you, Diary, but to me it felt like a mini miracle.

AVA THE AMAZED

Dear Diary,

Dad said he got an email from Misty Oaks Library and that the story contest winners have been posted online.

"All of them?"

"All of them," Dad said.

"Even the honorable mentions?"

"Of course," Dad said. "So I finally got to read your story, Ava. And I liked it. It was like a fable."

More like a libel! I thought and felt bad all over again that I'd based Queen Bee on Real Bea. Dad said, "Mom will want to read it too."

"Did the library email the parents of all the kids who won or got mentioned?"

"I bet Mrs. White emailed everyone in town!" Dad said. "Or at least everyone with a library card."

I felt so wobbly I had to sit down. I used to like picturing people reading my story, but now I just want the story to go away.

AVA

Dear Diary,

Nobody said anything about my story today. Maybe I'm going to get off easy after all?

At dinner, Dad asked, "What's an eight-letter word that if you keep taking one letter away, it will still be a word all the way down until it's just one letter?"

Mom, Pip, and I had no idea what he was talking about, so Dad got out eight index cards and wrote one letter on each. They spelled S T A R L I N G. Suddenly I understood what he meant, and I went first. I took away the L so it was STARING. Pip took away the A so it was STRING. Mom took away the R so it was STING. I took away the T so it was SING. Pip took away the G so it was SIN. Mom took away the S so it was IN. And I took away the N and it was...drum roll please...I!

STARLING, STARING, STRING, STING, SING, SIN, IN, I! Cool, right? But then I started getting attacked by questions.

1. Did I commit a SIN?

2. Will I get STUNG?
3. Will everyone soon be STARING at *me*?

AVA...VA...A

11/10
BEDTIME

Dear Diary,

Nothing bad happened today either, so I showed the word-bird trick to my language arts class. They liked it.

Chuck had a trick too. He made a boxer's fist and wrote M, E, A, and T under his knuckles so his fist said MEAT. Then he lifted his pointer finger, so his fist said EAT. He put it down, so his fist said MEAT again. Then he lifted two fingers, and his fist said AT. And then he opened up his whole hand and inside, he'd written JOE'S. He said, "Get it? EAT MEAT AT JOE'S!" (Maybe he should be a comedian instead of a boxer.)

Speaking of words, tonight, my family played a game of Boggle, and we added a new rule: double points for palindromes.

When I was really little, Mom and Dad used to give me points for one-letter words (like A or I) and two-letter words (like AN or IN). That made Pip mad because her words had to be at least three letters.

Now that I'm almost eleven, mine do too.

Well, I found S-E-E-S and E-Y-E and G-I-G and S-O-L-O-S and T-O-O-T. But so did everyone else, so those got crossed out. Mom and Dad both found L-E-V-E-L, so they canceled each other out. I got double points for B-O-O-B, which Pip thought was funny. And Pip got double points for B-I-B. I was tempted to tease her about being a baby with a B-I-B and P-U-L-L-U-P diapers, but when Pip acts babyish, it's worse for everyone. Plus, I'm trying to be *kind* of *kind*—like the sun. I'm on a kindness kick!

To tell you the truth, I'm also glad that Pip didn't yell at me (or tell on me) after Bea's visit. It's strange, but we're both sort of pretending it never happened.

During the game, Mom said, "Ava, I read your story at work today. I even showed it to Dr. Gross. We thought it was clever."

For a second, I felt really good. Then I remembered what I'd written, and I felt more like a big balloon soaring high in the air that gets pricked and makes a bunch of farty noises and becomes a deflated crumple of shriveled rubber, lying splat on the ground.

Mom changed the subject anyway. "And, Pip," she said, "Dr. Gross said you've grown up a lot and have a beautiful smile."

Well, Mom's boss never says anything nice about human beings, particularly children. He's better with animals, particularly furry ones. (Mom says he's not that great with reptiles.) Whenever Pip and I go to Dr. Gross's clinic, he looks at us suspiciously, as though he thinks we might turn off the lizard lights or open the birdcages or let the dogs loose. Every so often, he'll act nice and show us an X-ray of a rabbit or a dog tick under a microscope. But mostly he's a grump. Mom says Dr. Gross complains that it's hard to be a vet because regular doctors have to know about just one species but vets have to know about a lot of species.

Anyway, I figured it out instantly: Pip must have given Dr. Gross one of her smiles. And it must have worked!

AVA, ASTUTE

11/11 (A PALINDROME DATE)
AFTER SCHOOL

Dear Diary,

The doorbell rang. I put down *Charlotte's Web* (which is short), and Pip put down *A Tree Grows in Brooklyn* (which is long), and we let Bea in.

"Hi, Ava! Hi, Pip! How'd it go this week?" she said.

Pip stared at Bea as if she were deciding whether or not to smile at her. But Bea just started taking off her gloves, scarf, jacket, and bike helmet.

"It's ccccold out!" she said, and for some reason, that seemed to warm Pip up.

We talked a little about the wind and rain, and then Bea plunked herself on the sofa. "Want some gum?" she asked, and Pip and I each took a piece. It was raspberry mint, which is my favorite after bubblemint.

"So who'd you smile at?" Bea asked Pip with a smile.

"A few people."

"A few? Or seven?"

"Five."

"Well, spit it out…"

I imagined Pip spitting (yuck!), but Pip started to answer. "Let's see, on Thursday, I smiled at Ava's friend Maybelle. On Friday, I smiled at the gym teacher, but I don't think she noticed. On Saturday, I smiled at our postman. And on Monday, I smiled at my mom's boss, and he actually told our mom."

"Positive reinforcement!" Bea said, and I wondered how positive she was going to feel once she found out that our stories had gotten posted online.

"On Tuesday," Pip continued, "I smiled at a girl, Nadifa, who just moved here from Somalia. She smiled back and sat by me at lunch. But it was a little awkward because neither of us knew what to say."

"No one ever died of awkwardness," Bea said. "Overall, how did it feel?"

"Overall, pretty good," Pip admitted.

"You think you can keep smiling this week and do a whole new assignment?"

"Depends on the assignment," Pip said.

"Here it is. When you see your reflection in a mirror, I want you to say, 'You are totally awesome!'"

"No way!" Pip said.

"Yes way. But don't worry, not loudly! Mostly just say it to yourself. Or say it in your head. It'll boost your confidence."

"My confidence?" Pip repeated. "No. Sorry. I can't. I really can't."

"Yes, you can! You can do anything!"

"I'd feel too stupid." Pip looked at me for backup, but I stared straight down at my shoelaces.

"Never question your life coach," Bea said. "It may sound weird, but it works. Instead of letting shyness conquer you, you have to conquer it!" She handed Pip the second strip of yellow paper.

Pip looked at me and read the words aloud:

Week Two:
Every time you see your reflection, tell yourself, "You are totally awesome!"

She rolled her eyes, so Bea added, "If you'd rather give yourself a specific compliment, like 'I draw well,' or 'I'm good in school,' that would be okay too."

Pip shrugged, and Bea shrugged back, so I shrugged too.

"I'll try," Pip said softly, and I wanted to jump up and down shouting, "Y-A-Y!"

"Great," Bea said. "Okay, same time next week!" She started putting back on her gloves, scarf, jacket, and bike helmet, and then got on her bike and rode off.

When she was out of sight, Pip said, "Seriously, Ava, why couldn't you have just minded your own business?"

I didn't know whether to say, "I don't have a business," or "C'mon, it's kind of working," or "Can't you see I have worries of my own?"

So I pulled a Pip—I kept quiet.

Ava, Agitated

11/11 (STILL A PALINDROME!)
BEFORE DINNER

DEAR DIARY,

I heard Pip talking in her room, so I slowed down by her door.

Here's what I heard: "You are totally awesome."

I thought that was funny (H-O-H-O-H-O-H) and was tempted to call Maybelle. But I decided not to, even though Maybelle and I usually tell each other everything. (In first grade, she was the first person I told when I got lice, which Pip says I called "head lights.")

Thing is, if I tell Maybelle about what's going on, Pip might kill me, and I'm big on life. Besides, I'm also trying to be a kinder, better person.

I'm glad I can at least tell you that I am—

AVA THE AMUSED

DEAR DIARY,

Mr. Ramirez just said, "I read your story online, Ava. The link went out to all the regional schools and town libraries." He also told me that Mrs. (Bright) White nominated it for a nationwide contest for a book called *Kids' Eye View: Short Fiction by Young Writers*.

"Why?" I asked, though he probably expected me to say W-O-W or Y-A-Y.

"Why? I imagine she liked it! And if your story becomes part of a collection, that brings recognition not just to you, but to the entire Misty Oaks School District."

Here's what I did *not* say:

1. "I wish you'd never told me about the stupid contest."
2. "Help! I wrote a mean story about a nice person!"
3. "My stomach hurts. Can I go see Nurse Abrahams?"
4. "Am I really a 'Young Writer'?"

Here's what I did say: "Did she nominate other stories too? Like 'Bookshop Cat'?"

"No, just yours," Mr. Ramirez answered.

"I don't think I even want to win," I mumbled, imagining all my words on the loose in cyberspace.

"Why not?"

I didn't answer, but I wondered if he would figure it out. After all, he'd been there when Bea and I had our meetings and made the Pip Pointers.

AVA, ASHAMED

Friday the 13th
bedtime

Dear Diary,

I do not believe that unlucky things happen on Friday the 13th. I believe that bad and good things happen all the time. Sometimes they just do, and sometimes people do dumb stuff or smart stuff that makes them happen or not happen.

I also doubt one pen is luckier than another. And I know pens can be replaced and don't really and truly have magical powers. But I still wish I hadn't lost the pen Dad gave me. When I wrote with it, it felt as if Dad were right there helping me or, I don't know, rooting for me.

Anyway, Mom said Nana Ethel has laryngitis and "lost her voice."

I said, "I hope she finds it."

Mom didn't laugh.

I'm still hoping I can find my voice. I know it didn't get "lost" like my pen, but is it the kind of thing you can find—ah-ha! (A-H-H-A)—like a four-leaf clover? Or is it something you have to discover little by little?

Yesterday, Dad was helping a high school senior write his essay for college. They were in the dining room reading out loud. It started out like this: "I feel fully prepared to undertake rigorous academic challenges."

I thought that sounded good, but Dad said, "Can you put more of your personality in there, Taylor? Let them hear your voice." He even added, "Kids think about how they look, but not how they sound."

The whole voice thing still confuses me. I know it's more than tra-la-la-la-la, but what is it?

Being a writer is way more complicated than I ever thought.

To tell you the truth, I started feeling a little *overlooked* as I *overheard* Dad tutoring Taylor. Dad was so full of en*courage*ment, and I don't think he gets that I need extra *courage* too. And that a little attention would go a long way.

Bea and I have been encouraging Pip with the Pip Pointers, but I wish Mom and Dad realized that I could use some advice too.

Do they need Parent Pointers??

AVA, ABANDONED?

11/14
BEDTIME

DEAR DIARY,

We went to The Great Wall for dinner. It was raining, and I said I liked the sound of the raindrops on the sunroof.

"*Rain*drops on the *sun*roof," Dad repeated. "That's almost a poem."

When we sat down, we ordered egg rolls and dumplings, and I looked at the menu and said, "Wonton? Not now." Then I spelled it out: W-O-N-T-O-N-N-O-T-N-O-W.

Pip said, "Good one, Ava!"

Dad laughed, and I liked that they appreciated my wordplay. It made me want to keep playing with words.

Pip went to the bathroom, and I followed her. I wanted to ask her how things were going with her crush, but she was blabbing away about how she and Nadifa are going to be lab partners. (*Blab* partners??) Well, Pip was so busy talking about science experiments that she didn't notice that Mrs. (Bright) White walked in behind her—and *between* us.

Mrs. (Bright) White didn't notice me either, and I didn't say anything because it's awkward to see a librarian outside of a library. Especially in a bathroom!!

What was really awkward was what happened next.

Pip marched up to the mirror, fluffed her red hair, smiled, and proclaimed, "You are totally awesome."

Mrs. (Bright) White said, "Excuse me, are you talking to me?"

"No!" Pip replied, all flustered. "I thought you were my sister!"

"Your sister?" Mrs. (Bright) White turned and saw me hiding in the doorway. "Oh! Hello, Ava!" She looked back at Pip and said, "I quite agree: Ava *is* awesome." She smiled and added, "And how nice that you two get along so well."

Pip and Mrs. (Bright) White went into separate stalls, and when they came out, they washed their hands side by side like it was no biggie. I just stood there wriggling, because I was not going to pee with Mrs. (Bright) White in the room!

They left, and after a minute, I left too.

Guess what? Mrs. (Bright) White was at our table talking to Mom and Dad! She was telling them that she sent my story to the publishers of *Kids' Eye View*. "I think it has a real chance in the fifth-grade category," she said.

Mom and Dad smiled, and I tried to. But as Pip knows, sometimes even a *little* smile takes a *big* effort.

AVA, AWKWARD

DEAR DIARY,

After breakfast, I went to Maybelle's. Maybelle's mom congratu-lated me about the writing contest, and I mumbled thank you. I still hadn't told Maybelle about the Pip Pointers or my Queen-Bee-Real-Bea worries.

We went to her backyard, and she said, "Want to trim my hair?"

I said, "I've never trimmed hair before."

"Yes, you have," she said. "Remember when we gave haircuts to all of Pip's Barbies?"

Actually, I still feel kind of bad about the time we pretended we had a barbershop. It was a long time ago, but Pip got really upset when she saw all the yellow Barbie hair on the floor of our basement. Mom and Dad got mad too, so it's something I try to forget. But when you try to forget something, you usually remember it extra.

"We didn't exactly do a great job," I reminded Maybelle.

"That's true," she admitted. "But we're older now. And how hard can it be to trim hair?" She lifted a strand of her hair and examined the ends. "The thing is, at my mom's salon, they always cut off way too much."

She handed me scissors, and I objected a little more, and she said, "C'mon. Just snip off half an inch."

I protested, but she begged, so I started: *snip, snip, snip.*

(Funny: *snip, snip, snip* backward is *pins, pins, pins.*)

I was nervous but not *pins*-and-needles nervous, so I kept doing it, cutting Maybelle's hair. At first it came out a little slanty: the right side was longer than the left. I said this out loud, and Maybelle said, "Just even it out."

I tried, but then the left side was longer than the right. "That's okay. You can fix it," Maybelle said, so I tried. I was getting a little worried though. What if I kept evening it out until there was no hair left? Fortunately, that didn't happen. But all in all, I ended up cutting about *four* inches—not half an inch. And it still wasn't completely even.

"I'm sorry!" I said.

She said it was okay, and I blurted, "Want to trim my hair?" I don't know why I said that, because I didn't even need a haircut. But before I could take it back, Maybelle said, "Sure."

Next thing you know, she was behind me chatting and snipping.

"I meant to tell you," Maybelle began, "the other day in school, Pip smiled at me."

"Really?"

"Really. And in the lunchroom last week, I saw her sitting with a new kid, *laughing.*"

Well, next thing you know, I told Maybelle everything. When you're not *facing* someone *face*-to-*face*, it's easier to spill your guts. (Yucky expression.)

Thing is, I needed to talk, and I knew I could trust Maybelle with my secrets—I was trusting her with sharp scissors at my neck!

When I was done explaining everything, she said the Pip Pointers sounded cool and not to worry too much about my Bee-Bea story getting read by too many people.

"I hope you're right," I said, feeling better. I was tempted to tell her about Pip's crush, but resisted. Besides, I didn't want to distract her. "How's it going back there?" I asked.

"I'm just trying to even it out."

A little later, I said, "Almost done?"

"Almost."

For a few minutes, things were quiet. Then she said, "Oops."

"What??"

"Nothing."

"Nothing?" I knew it was *not no*thing, but I didn't want to add another worry to my list of worries.

"I'm on the finishing touches," Maybelle said. "Hold still."

"I'm trying!" I said, even though I was also trying to take my mind off my head, which is as hard as it sounds.

"Done!" Maybelle finally announced, sounding apologetic. She ran inside to get a mirror. I looked at all the curled wisps of brown hair on the grass. Mine was a little darker than hers.

When she came back, we checked each other out, front and back. We both looked worse instead of better, and we knew it.

"Is your mom going to be mad?" I asked.

"No. She hardly ever gets mad."

I felt a pang of jealousy, but a little bit of relief too. "Good," I said, because I would hate having a friend's mom mad at me!

"Is yours?" Maybelle asked.

"She might not even notice," I had to admit, and Maybelle looked a little sad for me.

"You know what we need?" she said.

"What? Hats? Wigs? Brown bags?" I was trying to be funny.

"Moonglasses!!" she pronounced and dug into her pockets. She brought out two pretend pairs and put hers on the movie-star way. I did too.

"Look!" she pointed up. "The moon! And the man in the moon!"

We looked, and in the middle of the blue sky, surprise! There was a big round white moon. That made me feel a little better—it was like the moon was watching over us or something.

"Is it really 24,000 miles away?" I asked.

"Multiply by ten!" Maybelle laughed. "*240,000* miles!"

AVA WITH ALTERED HAIR

11/16
AFTER DINNER

DEAR DIARY,

Mom and Dad went to a party and told Pip and me to "look after each other."

Pip asked about my hair, and when I told her, she said, "It'll grow back."

"I know," I said and nuked some alphabet soup.

I've liked alphabet soup ever since I was a baby. I used to eat it at room temperature in a high chair. I even have a poster next to my bed of a can of Campbell's alphabet soup. It's by Andy Warhol and is called P-O-P art.

If Pip keeps drawing, maybe she can make P-I-P art.

Tonight, all Pip made was a mess. She poured herself some Lucky Charms, and then her cell phone buzzed—practically a first. It said: "Nadifa." Pip jumped up and—*unlucky* for her—spilled the *Lucky* Charms.

On the floor was a pink puddle of soggy shamrocks, pots of gold, shooting stars, rainbows, and mushy hearts.

"Smooth!" I said, but Pip just picked up her phone with one hand and a sponge with the other. Last week, she might have cried over spilt milk. Today she mopped up and kept talking.

"Tomorrow? Sure!" Pip said into the phone. "I love ice-skating!"

I stirred my letters, looking for words and keeping myself company. It's not that I expected Pip to include me. But I didn't expect to feel left out.

AVA WITH NO APPETITE

Dear Diary,

Dad told me he'd googled "Wren Misty Oaks" and three of his plays popped up. "So did 'Sting of the Queen Bee,'" he said. "There are two writers in town now!"

"I never thought my story would show up online," I mumbled, quiet as Pip.

"Well, no need for modesty. The more people who see your work, the better." He put his arm around me. "Maybe it'll go viral!"

"Like a virus?" I asked.

Dad laughed, but I didn't.

I wished I could tell him that even though "Sting of the Queen Bee" got an *honorable* mention, it's making me feel like a *dishonorable* person!

No, worse. It's making me feel like P-O-O-P.

AVA, AILING

DEAR DIARY,

Yesterday, Maybelle's mom took her to get a real haircut, a "bob" (B-O-B), and today at school, everyone kept saying how adorable she looks. I tried not to feel jealous.

My math teacher, Miss Hamshire, stopped me in the hallway. Most kids refer (R-E-F-E-R) to her as Miss *Hamster*. She has beady eyes and big glasses, and no one likes her except Maybelle, because Maybelle loves math and Miss Hamshire loves kids who love math.

Miss Hamshire said, "Ava, I read your story on the school website. I hope it's not based on any fellow students." She peered down at me, her beady eyes all googly and magnified.

I started sweating, because I had a feeling that my math teacher had put 2 + 2 together.

"I wonder what Mrs. Lemons thinks," she said.

"Mrs. Lemons likes me," I blurted, which was moronic because Miss Hamshire hadn't said she didn't like me. She'd just hinted that she didn't like my story.

After school, Bea came over. Her hair was in a braid, and she asked about my hair. I told her, and she offered to try to straighten it, but I said, "No thanks." I mean, just because Bea is good at giving advice doesn't mean she's good at giving haircuts, right?

She turned to Pip and said, "How'd Week Two go?"

This time, Pip seemed happy to answer. "I won't give you a day-to-day play-by-play. But whenever I saw myself in a mirror or a window, I did what you said: I gave myself a compliment. Fortunately, only one person caught me—not counting Ava."

"And I don't count," I joked, then realized that this was starting to feel a teeny bit true.

"Did you also keep smiling at people this week?" Bea asked Pip.

"Mostly at myself," Pip answered.

"Well, that's part of the whole point. But keep smiling at other people too. Not 24/7, and not when you don't feel like it. But sometimes, when you can."

"I'll try."

"Good. So you ready for your third assignment?" Bea pulled a folded strip of paper from her pocket and read it aloud.

Week Three:
Say hi to someone new every day, kid or grown-up.

"That's it?" Pip asked.

"That's it," Bea said.

"That doesn't seem so hard."

"It's not."

I almost pointed out that "It's not" sounds like "It's snot," but

I didn't. Funny how Pip has to tell herself to speak up and I have to tell myself to shut up. Just because something pops into my head doesn't mean it should leap from my lips.

Bea looked at Pip. "Two weeks ago, it would have seemed harder."

"You're probably right," Pip said.

"I *am* right," Bea said with a twinkle, and somehow it didn't sound conceited.

The phone rang. It was Mom. Pip answered and started talking, so I walked Bea out to her bike. "How'd you get so good at helping people feel more confident anyway?" I asked. It's not like she went to Advice Columnist School or Life Coach Academy.

"At my old school," Bea replied, "the whole sixth grade was pretty clique-y, and a lot of girls put me in the middle of their fights. I didn't like it, and there were a lot of stupid rumors. So I talked to my aunt a lot—she's a psychotherapist. She's expensive, but she always talks to me for free."

I started wishing I had an aunt who was a psychotherapist. But I don't, and even if I did, I couldn't picture myself talking about my troubles.

"I also just hung out at the bookshop a lot," Bea continued. "Me and Meow Meow. I read a ton: novels, magazines, and books with quotes."

"Quotes?"

"Quotes. You know, like, 'No one can make you feel inferior without your consent.'"

"Who said that?"

"Eleanor Roosevelt. And, 'The only way to have a friend is to be one.'"

"Who said that?"

"Ralph Waldo Emerson."

"You know a lot of quotes?"

"I guess. Oprah Winfrey said, 'Being angry with other people hurts you more than it hurts them.'"

I thought about how angry I'd been at Bea before I'd even met her. "The only quotes I know are the morals of Aesop's fables."

"The morals?"

"Yeah. Like, you know 'The Mouse and the Lion'? It's about a big lion that spares a little mouse, and later, when the lion gets captured by hunters, the mouse saves him by gnawing through the hunters' net."

"What's the moral?"

"No good deed, no matter how small, is ever wasted."

Bea nodded. I think we were both aware that we were doing Pip a good deed, but only I was aware that deed (D-E-E-D) is a you-know-what.

I started thinking about the moral of my Queen Bee story: "There's no shortcut to true friendship." Then I thought I'd been *right* about friendship, but *wrong* about Bea.

I wished I could tell her that I was worried that my BEE-BEA story was turning into a BB gun, but I couldn't.

Besides, Bea's visits aren't for me. They're for P-I-P.

AVA, AWARE

11/18
MIDDLE-OF-THE-NIGHT

Dear Diary,

I just got out of bed and turned on my lamp. I hope Mom and Dad don't notice and tell me to turn if off and go to sleep, but there's something else I want to tell you.

In gym we combined classes and this lady came to teach us yoga. She talked about "breathing" and "balance," and it was actually pretty calming. Then she said to pretend we were trees.

First, we stood on our right leg and lifted our left foot in the air and raised our arm-branches and wriggled our finger-leaves and tried not to fall. Then we switched and stood on our left leg and lifted our right foot in the air and raised our arm-branches and wriggled our finger-leaves and tried not to fall.

It was hard!

Most of us couldn't help wriggling and jiggling, and some of us (including me) kept putting our feet down so we wouldn't keel over. A few of us did fall!

Only Chuck had no problem standing perfectly still. I bet he could have stood there like a tree all day long. He's either extra coordinated…or part egret?

Well, the yoga instructor told us to form a circle, stand on one leg, hold hands, and make a "group tree." (She should have said "forest.") I was in between Maybelle and Alex, and as I reached for their hands, I started to giggle, but the instructor said, "No giggling, and please close your eyes."

Next thing you know, we were all in a circle with our eyes shut.

"Some of you are still swaying, like trees in a breeze," the instructor said. "But notice how you are holding each other up and supporting one another. Be aware that you can trust each other, and know that you will not let each other fall."

The amazing thing was: she was right! All of us (except Chuck) kept wobbling, but not one kid fell! Not one! Alex and I almost fell, but we both "supported" each other and even shared a teeny tiny half-smile.

Right now, under my covers, I'm thinking that even though my plate is chock-full of worries, and even though Pip can sometimes be annoying, I'm glad that Bea and I are helping her.

She's my sister, after all, and I'm not going to let her fall.

AVA WREN, YOGA TREE

DEAR DIARY,

Lunch was meatballs. Maybelle and I were standing in line right behind Pip, and I was starving to death (poetic license). Pip said hi to the lunch lady, and while I paid for my meatballs, the lunch lady, who is very bubbly, said, "Ava, I read your story about the bee! Good for you!"

I said, "Thanks," even though her "*Good* for you!" made me feel *bad* for me.

Well, Maybelle and I followed Pip into the lunchroom, and I don't know what Pip was thinking, but as she walked by two seventh-grade boys, *she said hi*. One was tall and skinny with curly hair, and the other was stocky with a starter mustache. Neither one answered—they just sort of looked through her.

Pip didn't even notice. She kept heading toward a corner table where Nadifa and Isabel were saving her a seat. The two boys were sitting next to Loudmouth Lacey. She's the girl with thick bangs and thick eyeliner who was mean to Pip last year.

Okay, I think this is a metaphor, not a simile, but let me put it this way: if middle school were an ocean, Lacey would be a barracuda and Pip would be a minnow.

Anyway, here's what happened. Lacey began making squeaky sounds, like, "Pipsqueak, squeak, squeak, squeak," and then the boys started doing it too!

At first, I couldn't believe my ears, but I stopped and listened, and it was true: all three of them were squeaking. Lacey was the loudest.

Maybelle and I were just yards away, and I was tempted to throw my meatballs at them. But what would that help?

Then things got worse.

Lacey took the rubber band out of her ponytail and twisted it around her tongue and lisped, "Look! I'm tongue-tied! I'm tongue-tied!" Mustache Boy cracked up, and soon all three of them were laughing like hyenas.

Personally, I couldn't take it anymore! How dare they make fun of Pip? I was glad she was at the other end of the lunchroom, and I was thinking how brave she had been to follow Bea's step-by-step advice and get herself "out there"—and how I should try to be brave too.

I started walking, step by step, toward their table.

Maybelle said, "Ava, no!" but it was like their table was a magnet and I was a paper clip. My heart was pounding, and my *sneakers*, instead of walking me safely away, were heading toward the *squeakers*. Suddenly I was standing in front of them, staring into the taller boy's eyes. I looked at him, human being to human being, and said, "Why can't you leave her alone?"

"What's it to you?"

"She's my sister!" I shouted, which surprised all of us, especially me.

Mustache Boy laughed, and Lacey lisped, "Sheeth her thith-ter!" But the tall boy was listening, I could tell.

"Give her a break," I said. "She's shy, but she's a good person." Mustache Boy snorted, and Lacey squeaked, and I added, "And being a good person is a good thing." I couldn't believe I added that.

I looked at Maybelle, and her mouth was flopped open. Other kids were listening too. Even Chuck. I wondered what would happen if a fight broke out. Would he jump up and defend me using his boxing and balancing skills?

The taller boy nodded at Lacey as if to say, "Let's stop," and Lacey made a face and mumbled, "Whatever." Then she stuck her hand in her mouth and slid the slimy rubber band off her tongue and shot it at the window, saliva and all. It struck the glass and fell onto the floor.

Mustache Boy shrugged, and they all stopped squeaking.

I just stood there, shaky as a one-legged yoga tree. I was trying not to drop my tray.

Maybelle got me to sit down, but I couldn't eat. I looked toward Pip. She and Nadifa and Isabel were all facing the wall. I was glad they had missed everything.

Funny, even as I write this, hours later, I'm still a little shaky. But I feel proud of myself too. Like, maybe for once, I blurted out the right thing.

AVA THE ADMIRABLE?

DEAR DIARY,

"Principal Gupta wants to see you."

These are six words you do *not* want to hear.

Since Principal Gupta never wants to see me, for a tiny second, I thought it might have to do with my standing up to the Squeakers. Maybe she was going to give me a bravery award?

But Mrs. Lemons wasn't smiling. And as I walked down the hallway and got closer and closer to Principal Gupta's office, I felt more and more sure that I was in trouble.

I knocked on her door, and she said, "Come in. Sit down."

I did, and I saw a blond lady sitting in the other chair. The blond lady looked familiar. I had definitely seen her before. But where?

Uh-oh! At Bates Books! And Misty Oaks Library!

"Ava, I'd like you to meet Mrs. Bates."

My heart went plunging down one of my legs and landed on top of my big toe. (Poetic license.)

"How do you do?" I said as politely as I could, but it came out kind of high-pitched.

Mrs. Bates eyeballed me as if she'd expected the malicious Ava Wren to be taller and tougher. "I've been better," she answered.

Principal Gupta said, "Ava, Mrs. Bates just read 'Sting of the Queen Bee.'"

My throat got all tight.

"I did," Mrs. Bates confirmed. "And frankly, I felt a little stung by it myself. I can't say I appreciated your portrayal of my daughter as an evil, selfish, rude friend-stealer."

I felt about as slimy as Ernie the Earthworm, so I apologized and said, "It was a mistake." I was tempted to mention Pip's ruined slumber party but decided not to, because Mrs. Bates hadn't asked what had *inspired* me.

"I liked 'Bookshop Cat,'" Mrs. Bates said, "and thought others might find it charming. So this morning I sent our customers an email with a link to the library contest site. Within the hour, two people emailed back asking me about Queen Bee, the nasty new seventh-grader. One even took it upon herself to telephone."

I sat there staring at the dark green rug. It had a bunch of crisscrossing vacuum lines in it. My eyes were prickling, and I had a lump in my throat.

"I'm all for free speech," Mrs. Bates continued, "but not when it's hurtful or damaging. At Bea's last school, she had to deal with a number of mean and jealous girls and their nasty rumors, and I don't want her to go through that again. That's why I came over to put an end to this."

"I wish I could press Undo," I mumbled.

"Speak up," Principal Gupta said.

"I wish I could press Undo," I repeated, a little louder.

"I wish you could too," Mrs. Bates replied. "Ms. Gupta, perhaps you can remove Ava's story from the school website? I assume that wouldn't be considered censorship?"

"Under the circumstances, I think it would be fine."

Principal Gupta phoned her tech person while I sat there like a criminal. I started feeling smaller and smaller, and it was all I could do not to burst into tears.

I thought: I wish my parents were here. Then I thought: no, I don't. And to be honest, that made me feel even worse!

"I'm not sure if Bea even knows about your story," Mrs. Bates said.

"She does," I said softly. "She and I already made up."

"Really? Well, I shouldn't be surprised." She nodded. "My daughter has a very forgiving nature. More so than I." Did that mean that Mrs. Bates was going to stay mad at me forever? "Bea is wise beyond her years, and she has a heart of gold."

I wondered what my heart was made of. Pebbles? Dirt? Mud? I was still afraid I might start bawling.

"Mrs. Bates," Principal Gupta said, "I feel certain that Ava has grown a lot because of this unfortunate experience. Would you say this is true, Ava?"

"Yes!" I said and threw in a couple more "I'm sorry"s. There was a silence, so I asked, "Would it be okay if I went back to language arts? I mean, if I'm not getting suspended?"

"It's okay with me," Principal Gupta said. Mrs. Bates gave a nod too, so I stood up and backed out of the room, closing the door behind me.

In the hall, I was starting to breathe full breaths again when a seventh-grader I'd never met before said, "Are you Ava Wren?"

"Yes."

"Bea Bates is a nice person," she said. "She did not deserve what you did to her."

"I know," I said and kept walking.

"What's with the weird hair anyway?" she called.

I hurried back to class wishing Thanksgiving were *this* week instead of next week.

AVA WHO WROTE A BUNCH (INSTEAD OF EATING LUNCH)

11/20
Friday afternoon

Dear Diary,

I don't know how Pip survives without talking. She may think talking is hard, but *not* talking is so much harder.

I wish I could talk to my parents the way some kids do. Or the way Bea talks to her aunt.

This afternoon, Maybelle and I sat in the library near Pip, Isabel, and Nadifa. Nadifa's hair is even shorter than mine, and she wears two earrings in one ear and one in the other.

Maybelle and I were playing I Spy. Here's what I spied with my little eye: Pip said a quiet hi to Bea's freckly brother! And Ben said a quiet hi back!

Questions:

1. Is Ben her crush??
2. Does Pip know that Ben is Bea's brother?
3. Does Ben know his mother hates my guts?
4. Does Pip have any idea about all the drama going on?

After the bell rang at the end of the period, I got up the nerve to talk to Mr. Ramirez. Since my story is no longer on the school website, I asked if he could ask Mrs. (Bright) White to take it off the town library website and also take it out of the running for the anthology. He said, "Why don't we call her together?"

I wanted to say, "Can't you just do it?" but he punched in her number. I was hoping a machine would pick up, but Mrs. (Bright) White said, "Hello," and Mr. Ramirez handed me the phone. I had no choice but to talk!

"Hello, this is Ava Wren, and I'm sorry," I said, apologizing to my third grown-up in one day. I admitted that I should have given more thought to my stupid story before handing it in and said, "I wish you could just make it all go away."

Mrs. (Bright) White said she couldn't "just make it all go away," but that she could remove the story from the library site. "May I ask why?" she said, and I had to tell her that I'd based Queen Bee on Real Bea in a not-nice way. "Well, that's a shame, Ava," she said. "When you have talent, you owe it to yourself and others to put it to good use."

I felt like a puppy who'd piddled on the carpet, but I said, "If you have a contest next year, I'll submit a story I can stay proud of." I hadn't expected to say that.

"All right, it's a deal. I'm looking forward to reading it already." It was funny that Mrs. (Bright) White was looking forward to reading a story I hadn't started thinking *up* or writing *down*. "And I'll notify the publisher that the author of 'Queen Bee' wishes to withdraw her story."

"Thank you," I said and added some more "I'm sorry"s for good measure.

Believe it or not, after I hung up, Mr. Ramirez apologized to *me*. He said, "Ava, I'm sorry this all got so out of hand and that we didn't discuss your story in the first place. In my day, kids could show poor judgment and their mistakes didn't go on their permanent record."

"This is going on my permanent record?!" I asked, horrified.

"No, no. I just mean, in the age of the Internet, you have to be extra careful. Mistakes can follow you around." I pictured my mistakes swarming after me like stinging bees.

I nodded, glad that at least Mr. Ramirez knows I'm *not* a bad person—I'm just a person who did a bad thing.

AVA WHO DOES *NOT* WANT HER MISTAKES TO FOLLOW HER AROUND

11/21
IN OUR CAR

Dear Diary,

Hi from the *high*way.

Dad and Pip and I are driving back from shoe shopping. Dad and Pip are up front, and I'm in the backseat—with you.

Bea called this morning and said, "Sorry about my mom."

I said, "It's okay." I told Bea that my runaway story had been taken off the school website and library website and that Mrs. (Bright) White had submitted it to be in a book, but I'd asked her to un-submit it.

"Wait. Why?"

"Because I want my story to disappear!"

"Wait a sec, Ava," Bea said. "I'm glad people in Misty Oaks won't be reading about the evil new seventh-grader named Bea, but I don't care if kids in Alabama or Alaska do. If you can get it published, you should."

"I don't know…"

"Well, *I* know. If Mrs. White thinks your story is good enough to get into a collection—"

"But it's *not*—"

"Never say no to yourself, Ava! Let other people do that for you. Because who knows? They might say yes."

I wondered if she'd gotten that from a quote book. "Too late," I said. "I already told her to withdraw it."

"So un-tell her! Let's un-tell her together! C'mon, we're biking to the library right now! I'm picking you up in five."

With Bea, there was no point in even protesting, and minutes later, we were pedaling to Misty Oaks Library.

I was hoping Saturday was Mrs. (Bright) White's day off, but she was at her desk wearing a cream-colored sweater speckled with maple leaves. I asked if she'd withdrawn my story, and she said she was "just about to do so."

"You can keep it in if you want," I said.

"Really?" She met my eyes. "What made you change your mind?"

I turned toward Bea. "Remember Bea Bates?" Bea took off her helmet, and her long blond hair came tumbling out.

"Of course! Hello, Bea. I love Bates Books, and I liked your 'Bookshop Cat' story—especially the bit about the fluffy orange cat who plays favorites among the customers. The competition among seventh-grade entries is quite stiff and…"

"Mrs. White," I said, "Bea thinks I should keep my story in the running."

"Really? May I ask why?"

"Bea is a very encouraging person," I said and looked over at her. Bea stayed quiet and gave me a smile.

"Well then," Mrs. (Bright) White said, looking at us in turn. "We'll simply leave everything alone and wait to see what the editors decide."

I thanked her, and we left. But here's the funny thing: I still don't know if I want my Queen Bee story to go into a book…or to just go away.

AVA, AMBIVALENT BUT WITH NEW SHOES

DEAR DIARY,

This morning, Bea came over and asked Pip if she'd been saying hi to a lot of people.

"Not a ton," Pip answered and looked at me. I could tell Pip was thinking of spelling out N-O-T-A-T-O-N, and hoped she wouldn't. I didn't want Bea to know how strange our family is!

I nodded to Pip, as if to say, "Don't," but then I was afraid Pip might tell me not to nod—and spell that out too: D-O-N-T-N-O-D.

Bea said, "I just mean: did you talk to someone new every day?"

"Yes," Pip said and mentioned the lunch lady, a substitute teacher, and a bus driver. She did *not* mention that some of her someones were boys, and that two did not smile back (in the lunchroom) and one did (in the library).

She also did not mention Ben by name. Is that because he's a boy or because he's Bea's brother? Or does Pip still not know? I'd thought of telling Pip, but since I wasn't sure if that would help or backfire, I didn't.

"Great job!" Bea said to Pip, and we snacked on pretzels.

After a while, Bea checked her cell phone and said, "Gotta go. My parents are waiting for me because we're going to my grand-parents' for Thanksgiving. I hope I don't get *ill* in *Ill*inois—get it?"

"Got it!" I said, surprised by her wordplay. "You won't!"

Bea handed Pip a fourth assignment.

WEEK FOUR:
COMPLIMENT ONE PERSON EVERY DAY—ON ANYTHING AT ALL.

After Bea left, I asked Pip if she still thought Bea was bossy. Pip thought about it and said, "Yes, but somehow I don't mind."

"Same," I agreed. Because Bea isn't really bossy. More like bold and encouraging and generous.

And she likes us—and we like that!

I went into my room and scooped up two handfuls of Mini M&M's then went into Pip's room with both hands behind me. "Pick a hand," I said.

Pip pointed. I opened my right hand and dumped the Minis into her palm.

"Yum!" she said. "Lucky guess!"

"Actually," I said, "lucky is having *me* as a sister!" I opened my other hand and showed her that it was also full of Minis. And I spilled those chocolates into her palm too.

AVA THE ADORABLE

Dear Diary,

I found another Pip note in my room. It said, "I know I'm lucky."
At first I was confused, then I realized she wrote it after I told her
she was lucky to have me as a sister.

Well, even though it's just four little words and not a bouquet
of roses, four words from Pip are a lot.

I was going to throw the note away, but instead I'm taping it
right here.

I know I'm lucky.

AVA THE ANGELIC

THANKSGIVING MORNING

DEAR DIARY,

As soon as we woke up, Mom said, "Kids, we have a lot to do before everyone gets here. Give me a hand in the kitchen."

Pip said, "Okay."

I said, "I don't mind helping, but I need both my hands." Mom didn't react, so I added, "I'll give you a hand if you promise to give it back." She still didn't crack a smile. (Do people crack smiles? Or only eggs?)

I wondered if Mom thought I had a bad attitude when I was just trying to be funny.

Finally I said, "What do we have to do?"

"Set the table for seven," Mom said. "With cloth napkins."

AVA WITH AN ATTITUDE?

11/26
Thanksgiving night

Dear Diary,

I'm as stuffed as our turkey was, but I'm confused too. My feelings are all jumbled.

Nana Ethel and Aunt Jen and Uncle Patrick flew in early, and everyone gave everyone *huge hugs*.

When Uncle Patrick and Aunt Jen got married, Pip and I got to be flower girls. Aunt Jen didn't want to change her name to Jen Wren, so she kept her own name, which is Jen Honoroff, which sounds like On or Off, which makes Pip and me laugh.

Anyway, Nana Ethel, Mom's mom, asked Dad how his writing was going. Dad said, "Oh, you know, this morning, I took out a comma, and this afternoon, I put it in again."

Uncle Patrick said, "Oscar Wilde!"

Dad said, "Bingo!" which is a weird word. (It's not like kids go around saying, "Bingo!")

Dad and Uncle Patrick both love talking about Irish writers. Uncle Patrick once told me about a bunch of monks who wrote one of the first books ever—the Book of Kells. Instead of paper, they used calfskin. Instead of ink, they used ground-up rocks and gems!

When Dad started preparing the turkey, Uncle Patrick asked, "Is the FOWL FOUL?"

Dad smiled and said, "The NOSE KNOWS." Then he asked Uncle Patrick to hand over some herbs.

"You're running out of THYME," Uncle Patrick said. "TIME to get some more."

Dad said, "Homonym jokes are NOT ALLOWED. At least NOT ALOUD."

They were playing the Homonym Game! I thought Pip and I had made it up, but I guess not. Dad once told me that his father was the original word nerd and "pun pal" of the family. So maybe *he* invented it?

"No one BEATS your BEETS," Uncle Patrick said.

Pip must have decided to use one of her compliments, because she said, "You guys are funny. Ava and I like homonyms too."

I was surprised, but Uncle Patrick looked *really* surprised. His bushy eyebrows shot up and practically met in the middle. I think he'd forgotten Pip could talk.

Next thing you know, he was asking Pip about her sketches and schoolwork, and she was answering, and they were having a normal-ish back-and-forth conversation. She even showed him her "portfolio," and he called her work "very accomplished." She showed him two book covers she drew for English, and he said, "You've always been such a good reader."

Well, I wanted him to know that I'm a good writer and I thought about showing him *Winning Words* or telling him about the *Kids' Eye View* competition, but forget it, no way. I also thought of showing him my spelling tests, but I didn't want to seem desperate. And since I hadn't told Mom and Dad about all my 100s, I didn't see how I could tell Uncle Patrick.

Still, it was *not* easy listening to him praise Pip to the skies.

Who knew that Pip would keep on soaking up all the attention whether people are worried about her or proud of her?

To tell you the truth, it's making me feel upside down.

∀Λ∀ (A-K-A A-V-A UPSIDE DOWN)

Dear Diary,

Thanksgiving is over and I'm still mad.

For starters, I did way more cleanup than Pip. I took out tons of garbage—turkey bones and yam peels and pumpkin cans—and *I* got treated like garbage! Well, not garbage exactly. More like Cinderella before the fairy godmother part. No one asked about my life or realized that I deserve some credit for the fact that Pip was blabbing away about hers.

I wanted to invite Maybelle over, but there's some prehistoric rule that Thanksgiving is only for families.

While Pip was at dinner chitchatting with our relatives, Mom kept asking me to refill glasses and clear away dishes. I could tell she didn't want to interrupt Pip. Pip would say something, and Uncle Patrick or Aunt Jen or Nana Ethel would say something back, and it was like a jolly little ping-pong game was going on while I was running around being "helpful."

You know what? I'm sick of being helpful!

Have Bea and I created a monster? Pipenstein?

I wish I could talk about all this because, not to use a bad word but…#-A-M-M-I-T-I-M-M-A-D.

At dinner, I started to feel like a volcano full of hot simmering lava.

At least I can get my feelings out in you. For a few minutes, I couldn't find you, and I thought I was going to lose my mind. (Lost: one pen, one diary, one mind…)

Ava Full of Lava

11/30
IN THE LIBRARY

DEAR DIARY,

I'm at a desk in the library looking over bonus spelling words like "nuisance," "stomachache," and "invisible."

Some kids think bonus words are a "nuisance" that give them "stomachaches." But I love bonus words. What I hate is feeling "invisible."

Oh! Pip just walked in! She's sitting near the water fountain with Nadifa.

Ben is three tables away. I wonder if he noticed her.

Whoa! He did! He's staring at her!

I don't think she sees him though.

Wait! She definitely sees him!!

I can tell because she looked right at him then turned away and started looking everywhere *except* back in his direction.

Oh! Oh! He's getting up! He's walking toward her! He's a few feet away! He's at her table! He's sitting down!!

OMG!! I have to check this out close-up!!

I'm back. I went to get a sip of water so I could eavesdrop. Here's what I heard:

Ben said hi. And Pip said hi back. Then Pip said, "I like your sweater."

Well, I couldn't believe it. And I *didn't* believe it. Because I don't think Pip likes his sweater. I think she likes *him*!!

AVA WREN, SPYING AGAIN

DEAR DIARY,

Bea came by and asked, "How was Thanksgiving?"

I was about to grumble a bit, but Pip chimed, "Great," and offered her a slice of leftover pie.

"Pip's Pumpkin Pie," I said, because last week Mrs. Lemons said alliterations are when a bunch of words start with the same sound.

Bea got a funny look, and then Pip said, "'*Desserts*,' I stressed," (D-E-S-S-E-R-T-S-I-S-T-R-E-S-S-E-D), which is a palindrome. I could tell she was about to launch into our parents' peculiar passion for palindromes, but fortunately Bea complimented Pip's pie and asked, "So how'd it go? Did you compliment people this week?"

"I complimented my dad's turkey," Pip said, "and my uncle Patrick's jokes and my aunt Jen's earrings. And it all went really well."

"Just fantastic," I mumbled and tried to remember the last time anyone complimented me.

"How about in school?" Bea asked.

"I complimented Mr. Ramirez's holiday book display. And a boy's sweater."

"A boy?" Bea asked, eyes wide.

"A boy!" Pip giggled.

Was she going to name names?

Pip turned to Bea, "Should I tell him I like him?"

Bea considered the question. "It's usually better to *show* not *tell*. At least that's what real advice columnists say."

"*Show* not *tell*? How do I do that?" Pip asked.

Bea said, "Just talk to him and smile and stuff. He'll figure it out. He'll be able to guess, and you won't have to spell it out."

"Our family likes to s-p-e-l-l stuff out," I was thinking. But I didn't say that. I didn't say anything. Just call me Ava the Absent.

"The problem," Bea pointed out, "is that once you put stuff in words, you can't take it back."

"I guess," Pip said.

"I know," I almost added because, well, duh!

"Pip," Bea said, "I was going to say that you've come out of your shell like a snail or a turtle. But I think you've come out of your cocoon like a butterfly."

"Me?" Pip asked.

"You!" Bea answered.

I sat there trying not to feel jealous of Pip Hannah Wren, Center of the Known Universe.

"What's my next assignment?" Pip asked.

"To ask people questions, at least one per day. And to listen to their answers."

"I can do that."

"Good. Because it's your last assignment." Bea handed over the final strip of yellow paper. "Ava came up with this one," she added.

I wasn't sure if I even wanted credit or not. I mean, I know I'm supposed to be happy for Pip the Butterfly, but I'm also frustrated for—

AVA THE ANT

DEAR DIARY,

Over 2,500 years ago, Aesop wrote a fable called "The Ant and the Chrysalis." "Chrysalis" is an excellent spelling word and the story goes like this:

One hot day, an ant came across a chrysalis that was near its time of change. The ant felt sorry for it because it was imprisoned in its shell. The ant thought, "Poor you. I can scurry anywhere and you can hardly even wriggle!" Later, the ant came back to the same spot, and the chrysalis was gone. The ant was puzzled, but suddenly he saw that he was being shaded and fanned by the gorgeous wings of a beautiful butterfly. The butterfly called down, "No need to pity me, little ant!" And with that, he flew far, far away.

The moral: "Appearances can be deceiving."

Question: Is Pip nearing her "time of change"? And did she really become a butterfly while I'm still a bug?

AVA (AND AESOP)

12/3
IN THE LIBRARY

DEAR DIARY,

After lunch, which was chicken fingers, I saw Bea at her locker, so I went over to say hi. The taller Squeaky Boy stopped by and also said hi. I looked up at him, and he looked down at me, and then he said, "Hey, kid," in a not-mean way. When he left, Bea said, "You know Josh?" So I spilled the story about Lacey and the Squeaky Boys, which, come to think of it, sounds like the name of a terrible band.

"Wow," Bea said. "You're braver than I thought."

"Or dumber?"

"No, Ava. Braver. You're a risk-taker."

"Me?"

"You," Bea said, and suddenly I did feel a little extra brave.

AVA WREN, RISK-TAKER

DEAR DIARY,

I like thinking of myself as a risk-taker, so I decided to take a risk. I mean, it always helps to pour my thoughts out into you, but somehow I knew I had to talk to Mom directly. So I went to see her, my insides as fluttery as if they were crawling with ladybugs. (Gross simile.)

When I got to Dr. Gross's, Mom was busy as usual. At least Butterscotch was thrilled to see me. So was a *sh*aggy *sh*eepdog named *Sh*ep who just got *sh*ampooed for fleas. And so was a calico cat named Fever whose owner is always dropping him off for "observation" even though Dr. Gross keeps telling her that Fever is fine. (Fever once got his tail caught in a drawer, so now he has just a short nub because cat tails don't grow back; only chameleon tails grow back. Mom says Fever's owner feels guilty because it was her fault the file drawer was open.)

Anyway, I waited as patiently as I could, but at 5:05, I passed Mom a note. It said, "Mom, we have to talk now."

I knew the conversation would be awkward, but as Bea once told Pip, no one ever died of awkwardness.

Mom glanced up, and from her expression, I swear, I think she was afraid I was going to ask her to explain puberty. (*Hellllo!* I'm a kid. I don't even have B-O-O-Bs!)

"What is it?" she asked.

When Pip and I were little, whenever we got fussy, Mom would say, "Use your words." Well, as Wilbur found out in *Charlotte's Web*, even a few words can make a giant difference. And I'd been saving up a humongous pile of words—so it was time for me to let them out.

"It's me!" I said. "Me! I'm here and I matter!" Next thing you know, it was like a dam inside me had broken. I couldn't stop talking. "Mom, you pay way more attention to Pip than to me. You can't even deny it!"

Mom sat there as silent as the Old Pip. "It's true!" I said. "You favor her! You always have! Sometimes you act like she's as fragile as an old canary. Other times you act like she can walk on water, like that dumb lizard. Maybe it's the whole getting born early thing, but that was a long time ago, and Pip is a big girl now!"

"You're taller."

"Oh, Mom, that is *so* not the point! She's thirteen! She's a teenager! And she's not as small as she used to be. Not as quiet either—in case you haven't noticed."

"I have noticed. I'm proud of her."

I took a deep breath so I wouldn't explode into a billion boiling lava bubbles all over the walls and ceiling. "You should be proud of me too because I've been helping her. And I am *totally awesome*!" It came out much louder than I meant, so I was glad the waiting room was end-of-the-day empty. No dogs on leashes or cats in boxes or upset pet owners.

"I *am* proud of you, Ava."

"You don't even know what I'm going to say!"

"Okay, go on." For once, I had Mom's full attention.

"First of all, will you admit that you favor Pip?"

"No. I love you both equally!"

"I didn't say 'love,' I said 'favor.'" Mom stayed quiet, so I did too.

Finally she said, "If it sometimes seems that I favor Pip—and I'm not saying I do—I suppose it may be because I worry more about her. She's older, but she struggles more than you do. She's our Early Bird, and she still doesn't really fly." She met my eyes. "Can you keep that to yourself?"

"Yes," I said, because it doesn't count that I'm telling you, my diary.

"I can see how this might have felt unfair, and I'm sorry," Mom continued. "Maybe you and I should have talked about it sooner. But I never meant to favor her, just protect her, encourage her. I wish she could be more like you: friendly and fearless." She looked up. "Is there any chance you could take it as a compliment that I *don't* worry about you as much as I worry about her?"

"Depends," I replied. "Is there any chance you could start noticing me more?"

"Absolutely." Mom smiled softly. "What's 'second of all'? And what did you want to say?"

I liked that she'd been listening and that she thought of me as friendly and fearless. "Well, you know my story about the new girl—"

"Yes, I tried to email it to Nana Ethel today, but for some reason, it wasn't online anymore…"

I told Mom that the girl who gave the party turned out to be a very nice person, and that appearances can be deceiving. I also told her that I had to apologize to the girl's mother, and the principal took the story off the school website.

My voice caught a little when I said all this, because I was remembering that in Principal Gupta's office, first I wished my parents were there and then I was glad they weren't.

Since Mom was looking right at me, I added, "Pip has her struggles, but I have mine too."

Mom's eyes got a little shiny when I said that.

"If I tell you something else, will you keep it to yourself?" I asked.

She nodded, so I told her about the five assignments and how when Bea started *coming over*, Pip started *overcoming* her shyness. I didn't tell her about Pip's crush, but I did tell her about Loudmouth Lacey and the Squeaky Boys. Mom looked pained during that part, but I said I stood up to them.

"C'mere, Ava," she said. "You've been a super S-I-S, haven't you?" She gave me a big hug, and I pictured myself as a hero in a book: Ava Wren to the rescue! "And Pip *has* been more extroverted lately," she added.

I didn't want the subject to switch back to Pip quite so fast, but I said, "Extra what?"

"Extroverted. Outgoing. Talkative. Last week, she told me she participated in class."

Mom said Pip had told her that a substitute teacher called on her and she'd answered. "A lot of the regular teachers have stopped trying to call on her," Mom admitted.

"She participated? That's incredible," I said.

"Ava, *you're* incredible!" Mom said and looked right at me. "Thank you for what you're doing. And for telling me about it. I'm sorry I let work and other things get me so distracted."

"Thank you for listening," I answered. Then I think we both felt a little embarrassed about all the thank-yous, even though it's nice to be thanked and Thanksgiving wasn't that long ago. "Mom, can you *not* tell Pip that I told you about Bea? She'll probably tell you herself sometime. And don't mention the Squeaky People either. It would just hurt her feelings. Plus, one of the boys might not be as bad as the other."

"I hear you," Mom said, and I felt like she really did hear me. "We'll both keep quiet. Mum's the word."

"M-U-M," I said.

Mom looked up and stroked my hair. "Hey, you could use a haircut, don't you think?"

"Sure," I said, like it was no big deal.

AVA THE ASTOUNDED

Dear Diary,

It snowed today! Big fluffy flakes that didn't stick.

Three weeks till Christmas. Four till my birthday.

January 1st is a new year *and* a number palindrome (1-1) *and* the day I turn eleven (also a number palindrome).

I was thinking about what to give my family and I thought: maybe I've already given them pretty good gifts. Pip needed to get a life, and I helped her get one. And now, not only is Pip happier, but Mom and Dad seem happier too.

Dad's in the next room humming.

Is "hum" an onomatopoeia? Mrs. Lemons says those are words that are spelled the way they sound. Comic book examples are "pow," "bang," and "wham." Animal examples are "meow," "buzz," and "quack." A cereal example might be "snap," "crackle," and "P-O-P."

I went into Pip's room and asked, "Pip, do you think you and I are word nerds, like Mom and Dad?"

"Yeah, we can't help it," Pip said. Then she told me that in Spanish, she learned that "*Yo soy*" (Y-O-S-O-Y) means "I am"—which means other languages have palindromes too.

I told her that I knew a word that was eight letters and had only one vowel.

"In English?"

"Of course in English."

"How can that be?"

"It just is."

"Give me a clue."

I made a fist and pointed right at my bicep, but she didn't get it. So I said, "It's hard to guess. It's STRENGTH."

She nodded like she was impressed.

I told her that in the library, Mr. Ramirez lectured everyone about the Internet. He said we should *not* give out personal info, *not* believe everything we read online, and *always* be respectful of others. "Think before you click," he kept saying. "Fortunately," I said, "he did *not* say what inspired him."

AVA THE INSPIRING

DEAR DIARY,

This morning, Pip and I got haircuts, or in my case, a hair-fix. I got a B-O-B, like Maybelle.

On the way home, a flock of Canada geese honked in a V above us, and Pip turned to me all serious and said, "Do geese see God?"

I said, "What are you talking about?"

She spelled it out: "D-O-G-E-E-S-E-S-E-E-G-O-D?"

"Good one!" I said.

After lunch, Maybelle, Lucia, and Carmen came over. The twins were both wearing red, and we started playing a four-person card game of "I Doubt It." But then Carmen had to go home. Lucia didn't want to stop, so she said, "Think you can get Pip to play with us?"

I said, "I doubt it," and everyone laughed. But it occurred to me that Pip hadn't acted like a sore loser for a long time and hadn't been hiding in her room as much either. So I knocked on her door and asked her to play with us, and she said, "Sure," and took Carmen's place. And instead of us doing Pip a favor, Pip was doing *us* a favor. Which was nice, to tell you the truth.

When she sat down, Lucia said, "You're in seventh grade, right?"

Pip nodded.

"Don't the seventh- and eighth-graders have a dance coming up?"

Pip said, "Yes," and blushed a little.

"Are you going?" Maybelle asked.

"I don't know," Pip said.

Maybelle sneezed and Pip said, "Bless you," and I started thinking I should write Ben a note telling him that Pip likes him and asking if he likes her. But then I thought: nah, it's better to think twice (or three times!) before putting some things in print.

A-V-A WITH A B-O-B

DEAR DIARY,

In the library today, I went straight into Spy Mode—A-K-A Keen Observation Mode.

Pip and Ben were on opposite sides of the room, sneaking peeks at each other. I kept watching them watch each other, and soon only two minutes were left in the period.

I wanted to jump up and shove them together. It was time for one of them to make a move!

Suddenly Ben stretched, stood up, walked toward Pip, and said, "Oh, hey, hi," as if he'd bumped into her by pure accident.

"Hi," she said, barely looking up.

Neither of them said another word. I wanted to shout, "Talk! Talk! Talk about music or sports or TV! Or the weather! Or anything at all!"

But it was like they had *talker's block.*

At last, Ben said, "I like your watch. What time is it?" This was a funny question since there was a wall clock right by the door.

Pip said, "1:59. Thanks. I got it for my birthday."

They fell silent again.

His eyes landed on her book and he said, "*Great Expectations.*"

"Have you read it?" Pip asked.

He said no, and Pip told him there was a character in it named Pip.

From the corner of my eye (not that eyes have corners), I could see Mr. Ramirez starting to take giant steps toward them. I knew he was going to ask them to "pipe down," which is how he says, "Be quiet."

Well, I couldn't let him ruin the moment, so I looked straight at him, human being to human being. And just like that, Mr. Ramirez stopped in his tracks. It was as if he read my mind and decided to do a good D-E-E-D and let Pip and Ben talk (or at least try to).

"Some of my friends are going to the dance on Friday," Ben finally stammered. "Are you?"

I thought P-I-P might P-O-P, but she stayed M-U-M.

Then she said, "I haven't really thought about it," which I knew was not true.

Then they both went quiet again! They were M-U-M as mummies!

I wanted to jump up and say, "Don't believe her! She *has* thought about it, and she's dying to go with you, you, you!"

The bell started to ring, and Ben managed to mumble, "Maybe we could go together."

Pip looked up and said, "K," very softly, and their eyes met for a split second, and then Ben went back to his seat.

Well, neither of them said another word, but I knew that

inside, they were both all melty. And I felt sort of proud of them, and proud of myself too.

If Pip's life were a book, this would be the start of a whole new chapter! And I helped her turn some important pages!

AVA THE ALTRUISTIC

Dear Diary,

Mrs. Lemons asked us to do some in-class creative writing, and instead of worrying or getting blocked, I just wrote and wrote as if I were writing in you.

I got so inspired that I wrote a three-page story called "Invisible Girl." It's based a little on me and a little on Pip, but not quite on either of us. The first line is: "Once there was a girl who could disappear at will." I read the story out loud, and my whole class liked it, including Chuck, all three Emilys, Pony Girl Riley, and of course Maybelle.

Tonight when Dad tucked me in, I showed him "Invisible Girl," and he laughed at all the right parts. "Ava, this is good!" he said. "I like it even more than the other one."

"Thanks."

"You're a real writer," he said. "You have the gift of gab."

I said, "The gift of what?"

Dad said there's a castle in Ireland, and millions of tourists climb its tower, lean over backward while a guard holds their legs, and kiss the Blarney Stone so they can get the "gift of gab" and become better talkers.

"Is that a G-A-G?"

"No, I'm serious."

"Is it scary?"

"No, it's fun!"

"Is it germy?"

Dad laughed. "Life is germy."

"So why didn't you take Pip?" I asked.

"County Cork is a long way from Misty Oaks!" he said.

"I think she's figuring out how to talk anyway."

"I think you're right," Dad replied. He ruffled my hair, and I knew Mom must have told him about our conversation. I thought he was going to say, "Good night," but he said, "Do you sometimes feel that way?"

"What way?"

"Invisible."

My eyes stung, and the tip of my nose got all tingly as though I'd had too much wasabi on my sushi. I blinked a few times then said, "Sometimes. Maybe. A teeny bit." I didn't want to hurt Dad's feelings, but then again, he was asking about *my* feelings.

Dad nodded. "Ava, I'm sorry. Next time I'm talking too much or joking too much or reading too much, speak up, okay? If Mom and I get sidetracked with work or Pip, just talk to us. Don't wait for an invitation. I want to know what's important to you and what's upsetting you."

"Okay," I said and blinked some more. "Dad?"

"Yeah?"

"I got another 100 in spelling. That's all I ever get. Nothing but 100s. The kids in my language arts class think I'm a genius because I can spell words like 'genius.' And 'invisible.' They're rooting for me to get every word right for the rest of the year. Even this boy Chuck who can't spell to save his life and wants to be a championship boxer." I was talking way too fast, but the words came flying out. "Dad, I'm the best speller in the entire grade. I'm, like, a *great* speller!"

Dad kissed me on the head. "You know something, Ava? You're a great daughter too."

I smiled. "It's good I never kissed the Blarney Stone."

"What do you mean?"

"You once called me a 'chatterbox.' What if I never stopped talking?"

Dad laughed. "You're a talker, but you know how to listen too."

He was about to turn off the light when I asked, "Can I write for a few more minutes?"

"Sure." He glanced at my diary and added, "Hey! You're almost out of pages, aren't you?"

"Yup," I said.

He left, and I wrote down our whole conversation. Then I heard his footsteps and a knock on the door. "It's getting late," he said, poking his head in. He added that in *Ulysses*, James Joyce coined the longest palindrome in the Oxford English Dictionary.

"H-U-H?"

"Tattarrattat. T-A-T-T-A-R-R-A-T-T-A-T. It means 'knock on the door.'"

"Can I write that down?"

"Okay, but then lights out in one minute."

"Okay."

"And by the way," Dad said, "I meant what I said."

"About 'lights out in one minute'?"

"About you being a great daughter."

AVA (WITH AN AWW)

DEAR DIARY,

Bea asked if we could meet at her bookshop instead of our house. She said her parents like her to make herself "useful during the holidays" by unpacking boxes, shelving books, helping customers, and wrapping presents. December is their busiest season.

"Okay," I said, even though I was *not* dying to run into her mom.

After school, Pip and I walked to Bates Books, and on the way, we passed Loudmouth Lacey. She actually squeaked—but just once. I pretended not to hear, and I think Pip really didn't hear, which, in its own weird way, might be lucky. (Maybe she'll always have minor "social issues"? Maybe Lacey will too??)

At the bookstore, I saw Mrs. Bates. At first I wanted to pretend I didn't notice her, but Pip said hi, so I had to say something. I thought of Pointer #4 and said, "I really like your bookstore. It's so cozy."

Mrs. Bates looked surprised. "Why thank you, Ava. Having a bookstore was my dream ever since I was your age. Of course I didn't know what a challenge it would be."

She laughed like we were old friends.

Bea came over and motioned for us to follow her to the back, so we did. She said she had something for us. I thought it might be gum, but she handed us two night-light pens that glow in the dark! If you click the tips, they light up! You could use them to write in the middle of the night if you woke up and didn't want your parents coming in!

When Bea handed me my pen, she said, "Ava, 'Sting of the Queen Bee' was *not* my favorite story in the world, but if you keep writing, someday maybe we can sell your book right here at Bates Books." She pointed to a bottom shelf. "We could shelve it next to E. B. White's."

I liked imagining my name on a bookstore book. I began picturing a kid picking up a book by Ava Elle Wren, and maybe even looking at the front and back and skimming the first page and seeing what it was about and how it sounded and how long it was.

I also started wondering if the pen Bea gave me might feel magical. Then I realized that, magic or not, it was wayyy cooler than the library pen Alex got for his Ernie the Earthworm story because it was proof that Bea and I really had become friends after all.

"Does your mom know you're giving me this?"

Bea said, "Yes."

"Did she say anything?"

Bea looked like she was deciding how to answer. "She said you're a 'young writer with a lot to learn.'"

I couldn't argue with that, and I was glad Mrs. Bates called me a "writer," just as Dad had. Lately I have been thinking about *becoming* a writer, but in some ways, maybe I already *am* one? All I do is write! Well, write and spell.

Bea turned and said, "Pip, you deserve a fancy pen too because you completed all five assignments."

Pip thanked her and clicked the little light on and off, on and off.

"How'd the questions go this week, anyway? Did you talk to anybody good?"

"As a matter of fact…" Pip began.

Just then I saw a blur of orange. Was it the tip of a tail? I remembered hearing about Meow Meow and blurted, "Was it a cat I saw?"

"Great one!" Pip said. "W-A-S-I-T-A-C-A-T-I-S-A-W!" I didn't respond, and Pip said, "Ava, that's an amazing palindrome!"

"Palinwhat?" Bea asked.

"Palindrome," Pip said. "A palindrome is the same backward or forward. Like P-I-P. Or A-V-A."

"Wow," said Bea.

"Or W-O-W," Pip said. "Our parents Bob (B-O-B) and Anna (A-N-N-A) named us Pip (P-I-P) and Ava (A-V-A)," she continued, "and now we're all four word nerds!"

For the first time in my life, I wanted to tell Pip to shhh, be quiet, pipe down, and *shut up*. Was I going to be sorry I'd helped Pip find her voice? Was Bea going to think our whole family was bonkers?

"But what are ya gonna do?" Pip added merrily. "Sue us? S-U-E-U-S?"

Right then, I swear, I wanted to evaporate. I actually *wanted* to be invisible.

But Bea just laughed and said, "My dad is weird about words too." She said he was into alliterations, and that her parents' names are Bill and Beth, and they named their kids Ben and Beatrice. "Hey, Pip, have you met my big brother Ben Bates, my BBBB?"

Out of nowhere, her BBBB appeared, holding a striped orange cat. At first, no one said anything. Then the cat meowed twice and jumped to the floor.

"That must be Meow Meow," I said.

"It is," Ben and Bea replied at the exact same time. Ben turned to Pip, and their eyes locked. I have to say, Pip looked extra pretty, and for a tiny second, I pictured them married with two freckled toddlers, one boy, one girl.

Bea was staring at them too. "I guess you two *have* met," she said.

Pip and Ben stayed M-U-M, and I figured it might help if their younger sisters weren't standing there breathing on them.

I scooped up Meow Meow and gestured for Bea to follow.

As we walked away, Bea whispered, "So the boy Pip had a crush on is…*Ben*?" I nodded and hoped she wouldn't mind that I hadn't told her earlier.

"They do have a lot in common," she said.

"True," I said and listed three things:

1. Freckles
2. Shyness
3. Totally awesome sisters

Bea smiled. "Think they'll go to the dance together? Ben's still a little shy."

"I know they will," I answered.

"Huh."

"H-U-H," I spelled out, then suddenly noticed a copy of "Bookshop Cat," framed and hanging on the wall. "Your story!"

"Yeah, my aunt framed it."

"The psychotherapist?" I'd never said that word aloud before.

"Yeah," Bea replied.

"Cool," I said and asked, "Bea, did Ben read my story?"

She shook her head. "He wanted to, but he couldn't find it online. So he asked me if I had the library booklet, and I said yes, but that I'd torn out your story and fed it to the shredder."

"And had you?" I said, surprised.

"The day I read it. Turning your dumb-head story into confetti made me feel better."

"You mean, even future advice columnists are human?"

"Yup." She laughed, so I did too.

AVA THE AWESOME

Dear Diary,

Mrs. (Bright) White called to say my story didn't get picked for the anthology after all. "That's okay," I said. To be honest, I was more relieved than disappointed.

Someday I hope I'll write a story that is so good, I'll *want* it to get published. And even framed!

Could that happen? You never know!

Hey, I just noticed something: *know* backward is *wonk*.

AVA WREN, WORD WONK

12/12
Saturday night

Dear Diary,

Last night, I was folding origami snowflakes and snacking on grapes when Ben came over to pick Pip up for the dance. She looked happy, and I felt happy for her—which, trust me, is way better than feeling annoyed by her or sorry for her or worried about her.

After they left, Dad took me to buy a new diary at Bates Books because this one's almost done. (Obviously!) I'm pretty proud of myself for finishing it—and not burying it in my dead diary graveyard.

I think Dad's proud of me too.

Funny how I haven't been scared of blank pages lately. I like writing in them about…*everything*! And while I miss my magic pen, I like my new pen. So long as I have something to write with, I'm okay. It's when I have an idea and don't have a pencil or pen or marker or crayon or keyboard that I go a little nuts.

Anyway, when we bought the diary, Mr. and Mrs. Bates were both there. They were talking about decorating their shop windows, and I offered to make them one hundred origami snowflakes. "Would you?" Mrs. Bates asked. "We could put them in the children's section."

I said "Sure," and that's what I did the whole time Pip was at the dance. It felt like "penance," which is one of this week's bonus words. It means making up for messing up. As I folded and folded, I pictured my snowflakes decorating their cozy bookstore.

Observation: when you buy books online, it's not cozy, there are no homemade decorations, and a cat never comes by to rub your legs.

This morning, when Pip woke up and came downstairs, I asked how the dance was, and she said, "Really fun." Mom, Dad, and I exchanged a look.

I said, "Did everyone have fun?"

Pip said, "Everyone except Isabel."

"Why not Isabel?" Mom asked.

"Because both her parents chaperoned."

Mom and Dad laughed. Then Mom said, "I'm going to get a manicure later. You girls want to come?" Well, that was an absolute lifetime first, so we said sure.

At the nail salon, the lady said, "Pick a color." Instead of picking out a polish by color, like a regular person, I kept turning over the little bottles to read the names. I didn't want to pick "Blushing Bride" or "Nude Attitude" or "Pinking of You" or "Gold Digger." I finally settled on "Life's a Peach." Mom liked "Life's a Peach" too, so now she and I match.

Back home, I was passing Pip's room, which is a total disaster area, and on her desk, I noticed the five yellow strips of paper crinkled up. I poked my head in and asked if I could have them.

"What for?"

"I don't know, to tape into my diary."

"Why?" Pip looked at me as if I were a kook (K-O-O-K).

"Souvenirs," I said, but to tell you the truth, they might come in handy someday. Like, what if I ever have to be a head life coach instead of a junior life coach? Or what if I ever need a Friendliness Refresher Course?

Pip shrugged and handed over the strips, and here they are, all taped in:

Week One:
Smile at one new person every day.

Week Two:
Every time you see your reflection, tell yourself, "You are totally awesome!"

Week Three:
Say hi to someone new every day, kid or grown-up.

Week Four:
Compliment one person every day—on anything at all.

Week Five:
Ask someone a question each day. Listen to the answer.

When she gave them to me, she said, "Just so you know, I'm never going to turn into a big ol' blabbermouth."

"Good," I said, "because if you turned into a big ol' blabbermouth, I'd have to pretend we weren't related."

After I said that, I realized that I used to sort of pretend we weren't related anyway, and I felt kind of ashamed about that.

Maybe the Pip Pointers and all my trials and tribulations have helped me be a better person too?

AVA, NEW AND IMPROVED

DEAR DIARY,

Ben texted Pip to ask if he could come over to borrow her copy of *Great Expectations*. Lamest excuse ever! His parents own Bates Books! And I bet he could have downloaded it!

Pip said, "Sure," then went crazy cleaning her room and giving it a makeover. She even put her stuffed animals into a giveaway bag (poor things!). She left only one on her bed: a goldfish named Otto (O-T-T-O). She named him for the goldfish in *A Fish Out of Water*. (My favorite P. D. Eastman book is *Sam and the Firefly*, which is about a firefly that makes words that get people into and out of trouble.)

Anyway, when Pip was cleaning up, guess what she found under her bed?

No…

Guess again…

No…

Nope…

My Irish pen!!! The one Dad gave me!!!

Y-A-Y-Y-A-Y-Y-A-Y-Y-A-Y-Y-A-Y!!!

I went running around the house jumping for joy, happy as a lark. (Question: are larks happier than wrens or starlings?)

Dad was happy too. He said, "A good writer should have a good pen."

Then he told me the expression "The pen is mightier than the sword." So I told him *sword* scrambled is *words*. He laughed and gave me a hug.

Pip said, "You should take better care of your pens, Ava. A lot of good things happened because of stuff you wrote."

"A few not-so-good things too," I mumbled.

"True," she replied. "But more good things." She was blushing, and I wondered if someday she'd tell me more about you-know-who who, just then, rang the doorbell.

I'll say this: I love having my magic pen back, but what I like most about it is that Dad gave it to me. And that he thinks of me as a writer, a real writer.

You know what else? Just as Pip found my pen (which in some ways wasn't 100 percent lost), I think I may have found my voice (which in some ways may have been inside me all along).

The key might be to know, in your heart and your head, what you want to say and how you want to say it, and then to just trust that it will come out *right* if you *write* and *write* and *rewrite* and *rerewrite*.

AVA, ASPIRING AUTHOR

P.S. Has my pen been under Pip's bed ever since we played Word Scrambles on her floor? That was in *September*! (I know because I left the blank page in my diary.)

DEAR DIARY,

We hung up our holiday wreath. It has pinecones and a red bow and smells like Christmas.

At dinner, I mentioned that I got another 100 in spelling. Dad said, "You're unstoppable!" Pip joked, "GO, AVA, OG!" Mom said, "Great job, honey!" then added, "Can you spell veterinarian?"

I said, "V-E-T-E-R-I-N-A-R-I-A-N."

She said, "W-O-W," so I asked if they knew how to spell the longest word in the English language.

Mom said, "I don't even know what the longest word is."

Dad said, "Antidisestablishmentarianism?"

Pip said, "Supercalifragilisticexpialidocious?"

I said, "*Smiles*—there's a *mile* between the first and the last letter."

Mom and Dad laughed. And the funny thing was: that joke wasn't even that funny. So I told them a funnier one:

"Question: What does a fish say when it swims into a concrete wall?

Answer: Dam!"

They liked that one, so I figured this was a good time to show them what I'd made this morning. I'd found another lion and put it in a jar and added corn oil. It didn't come out as cute as Slimy Simba I, but Slimy Simba II was still cute. I held it up and asked, "Who can guess what this is?"

Dad looked confused.

Pip asked, "W-A-S I-T-A-C-A-T-I-S-A-W?"

"Close!" I said, because it was a palindrome and a feline. "Any other guesses?"

"A-H-A!" Mom said. "I know. It's a L-I-O-N-I-N-O-I-L!"

"Bingo!" I said just to be funny.

"I'm putting this on the windowsill," I announced. "Don't anyone throw it out." I looked straight at Mom.

"Wouldn't dream of it," she said. Later, as we were washing dishes, Mom said, "Ava, we still have a little time, but you and I should start planning your birthday, don't you think?"

"Sure," I mumbled with a shrug. But inside I started doing a happy dance.

AVA THE APPRECIATED

P.S. Pip just slipped two pieces of paper under my door. One is a sketch of me writing in you. It makes me look much older than ten. I look eleven at least. Maybe even eleven and a half. The other is a note. It says: "If there were a contest for Best Sister, you'd get First Prize."

You know what? I'm taping that right on my wall!!

12/21
AT 10:01

DEAR DIARY,

I hope I never lose my long-lost pen again. I hope I don't lose the one Bea gave me either.

I'm going to end this diary now, on a palindrome date at a palindrome time. I'll even throw in a palindrome sentence that Dad told us. It is perfect for today, the first day of winter, but it's a *word* palindrome (not a letter palindrome). Here it is: "Fall leaves after leaves fall."

Cool, right?

Well, it's late, so I'd better catch some ZZZZZZZs.

Wait, I just remembered: I wanted to end this diary with a moral.

First I was considering "Families and friends *count*—and a few even *spell*." But that's not really a moral.

Then I was considering "When you lose something, you find something," because I lost my pen and found my voice. But that's too fortune-cookie-ish.

Then I came up with a moral that's a little *sappy* and a little Ae*soppy*. Ready? Set? Here goes:

Moral: Helping others helps you too.

X-0-X-0-X
ABSOLUTELY AVA

Psssst, it's past midnight, and I just clicked on my new night-light pen. I wanted to see what it's like to write in the dark. Answer: totally awesome! My pen is shining a bright little beam onto my letters and words and putting them all in a spotlight—where letters and words belong!

I've been thinking a lot about pens lately—my Irish pen and my turquoise pen and my light-up pen—and how any pen can be a special pen. Or a power pen. Or a magic pen!

In one of my favorite picture books, *Harold and the Purple Crayon*, what's special isn't really the crayon. It's Harold's imagination. And the author's!

Funny, when you stop and think about it, it hardly even matters what kind of pen you use—or lose! What counts is what you write and think and not the color of your ink. (Hey, that's a poem!)

Anyway, the main reason I got up is that I have been thinking a lot about everything, backward and forward, and I have two things to say:

1. My family *is* seriously nutty. Maybe even extra-chunky-peanut-butter nutty. But they're mine, and I'm not going to trade them in. Not P-I-P. Not M-O-M. Not D-A-D. We're the Wrens, after all. And you know what they say about birds of a feather. (They stick together!)

2. I want to write a book someday. A book that kids my age can read and reread and even *reread*. That is my goal, and I'm putting it in ink right here right now: when I grow up, I want to be an author and write a book—a short one. I've been thinking that it could be about a good kid who does a bad thing and sometimes feels invisible, but who helps her sister find her voice and ends up finding her own. H-U-H. Maybe it could be a diary…

Here, in order of appearance, are the palindromes in this book:

AVA

MOM

DAD

PIP

HANNAH

ELLE

WOW

ANNA

BOB

HUH

EVE

MADAM I'M ADAM

MA HAS A HAM

SIS

POP

PUP

LION IN OIL

NAN

VIV

SENILE FELINES

SAGAS

STAR RATS

XOX

YAY

ATTA

MMM

STEP ON NO PETS

A MAN A PLAN A CANAL, PANAMA

KAYAK

RACE CAR

PEEP

RADAR

DUD

FUN ENUF

'TIS IT

NOW I WON

TOP SPOT

REDDER

A TOYOTA'S A TOYOTA

NO MELON NO LEMON

AHA

EVIL OLIVE

YO, BANANA BOY

LONELY TYLENOL

SOS

REPAPER

M&M

PEP

NOON

SEES

EYE

GIG

SOLOS

TOOT

LEVEL

BOOB

BIB

PULL UP

HOHOHOH

AHHA

WONTON NOT NOW

POOP

REFER

DEED

NOT A TON

DON'T NOD

AKA

#AMM IT I'M MAD

DESSERTS I STRESSED

MUM

YO SOY

DO GEESE SEE GOD?

GAG

TATTARRATTAT

WAS IT A CAT I SAW?

SUE US

KOOK

OTTO

XOXOX

And here are 15 bonus palindromes:

DOG DOO? GOOD GOD!

NEVER ODD OR EVEN

A NUT FOR A JAR OF TUNA

LIVE NOT ON EVIL

MY GYM

PARTY BOOBY TRAP

REWARD DRAWER

SPACE CAPS

HE DID, EH?

BORROW OR ROB

LLAMA MALL

MADAM, IN EDEN I'M ADAM

NOT A BANANA BATON

ABLE WAS I ERE I SAW ELBA

and

IN WORDS, ALAS, DROWN I…

Acknowledgments

I'd like to give a heartfelt shout-out to my early readers including kids, teachers, librarians, pros, friends, and family: Emme, Lizzi, and Rob Ackerman, Marybeth and Cynthia Weston, Denver Butson and Maybelle Keyser-Butson, Geraldine Rijs, Sandy and Stephanie Jenkins, Mary Lemons, Sue Hipkens, Carrie Silberman, Elise Howard, Sam Forman, Maureen Davison, Kelsey Allan, Nora Sheridan, Suzy Weiss, Anna Umansky, Olivia Framke, Cathy Roos, Lucie Aidinoff, Kathy and Ally Lathen, Anna Abrahams, Char and Clay Ezell, Laura Peterson, Elena Mechlin, Sinclair Target, Hannah Eisner, Karolina Ksiazek, Sydney Gabourel, and Max Lerman. Hurray for Trinity School in N.Y.C., Maret School in D.C., the Squam Lake family, Ragdale Foundation, and the New York Society Library where I'm lucky enough to be a judge of the annual Young Writers Awards. I'm hugely grateful to Susan Ginsburg and Stacy Testa of Writers House, and profoundly pleased that Steve Geck deemed Ava Jabberwocky-worthy, and that Victoria Jamieson, Jillian Bergsma, Derry Wilkens, and Cat Clyne all helped turn simple words into a beautiful book.

Don't miss Carol Weston's
Ava and Taco Cat

READ ON FOR A SNEAK PEEK!

12/28

DEAR BRAND-NEW DIARY,

I'm really worried. At dinner tonight, Mom said that right before closing, a man came into the clinic with an injured cat. He'd found him shivering in a tree! The cat was scrawny and scared and his neck had a gash and his left ear was bitten up. The man got the cat down and took him to the nearest vet—which was Dr. Gross.

"Poor cat!" I said.

"Is he going to be okay?" Pip asked.

"I don't know," Mom said. "Dr. Gross stitched him up and gave him antibiotics. If he makes it through the night, we'll call the shelter in the morning."

"*If!?*" I said.

Mom nodded. "I think a coyote got to him."

"What's his name?" Pip asked.

"No idea. But he's neutered, so he's not feral." Pip and I know that "feral" means wild, and "neutered" means he can't make baby cats. But does Mom know that stories about hurt cats and dogs make me sad?

"What does he look like?" I asked.

"He's honey-colored," Mom said. "But his right leg and paw are white, and he has a white zigzag above his nose."

"Awww," I said, trying to picture the cat's sweet little zigzag.

"No chip or collar or anything?" Dad said.

"No identification at all," Mom said.

Soon Mom and Dad and Pip were talking about other things, including dinner, which was stuffed eggplant—*blecch*! (Dad just started a terrible tradition of "Meatless Mondays." Fortunately, tonight he also made plain bowtie noodles for me.)

Well, I couldn't stop thinking about how lonely that cat probably felt all by himself in a cage at Dr. Gross's. I wished we could go check on him. But no way would Mom agree to go back to work after she'd already come home and put on her slippers.

I was trying to imagine what it must have been like for the skinny cat when the coyote started attacking him. He must have known it was life or death. He probably thought he was a goner for sure! It was lucky he was able to scamper up that tree, but then he must have been too afraid to come back down! And maybe too weak? I bet he was starving as well as stuck and petrified! Poor little thing!!

Suddenly my nose and eyes started tingling. I blurted, "May I be excused?" but it was too late! Teardrops fell right onto my bowtie noodles.

"Are you *crying*?" Pip asked, surprised.

"Oh, Ava." Mom met my eyes. "I'm sorry I brought it up."

Dad gave my hand a squeeze, and I ran upstairs and splashed

water on my face. I don't know why I was getting so upset about a lost honey-colored cat. But I was. I *am*.

It's just so sad to think of him all alone in a cage instead of a home.

Ava, Upse

A LITTLE LATER

After dinner, Pip came and knocked on my door, which was nice of her. She's been easier to talk to now that she's an official teenager. I think it's because she's been coming out of her shell instead of staying scrunched up inside it.

Anyway, she said, "Want to do another page?" so I said sure. Pip and I started making a book on the third day of winter break when we both got bored at the exact same time. I'm the author and Pip is the illustrator.

I'd wanted us to write *A Duck Out of Luck*, but I couldn't come up with a plot. Then I suggested *A Goose on the Loose*, but I couldn't come up with a plot for that either. Finally we decided to make an alphabet book because alphabet books don't have plots. I said it could be about animals, but Pip said it should be about fish.

Pip is constantly doodling fish. Her favorite stuffed animal is an orange fish named Otto. She named it Otto for two reasons:

1. O-T-T-O is a palindrome. It's spelled the same backward and forward, like A-V-A and P-I-P and M-O-M and D-A-D.
2. Otto is the name of the fish in *A Fish Out of Water*, which was the first book Pip read all by herself. (She has now read about a bazillion books.)

So far, our book is two pages long. It's called *Alphabet Fish*, and these are the two pages:

A is for angelfish.

The shy little angelfish has fins like wings.
Shh! It is hiding among weeds, rocks, and things.

and

B is for bumblebee fish.

If you found this fish, would you name it Bumblebee?
It doesn't buzz or sting, but it's black and gold, you see.

Pip has already made a list of the twenty-six fish she wants us to do. C was supposed to be for clown fish, but I thought about the lonely injured cat and said, "C should be for catfish." Pip agreed and drew a cute catfish with pointy whiskers.

I'm going to sleep now. I hope the lost cat is already asleep. What I really hope is that he makes it through the night!

AVA...ALMOST...ASLEEP

P.S. If I cross my fingers for luck, will they stay crossed while I'm asleep?

About the Author

Carol Weston lives in Manhattan. Her first book, *Girltalk: All the Stuff Your Sister Never Told You,* was published in a dozen languages. Her next eleven books include *The Diary of Melanie Martin* and three other Melanie Martin novels. Carol studied French and Spanish comparative literature at Yale, graduating summa cum laude. She has an MA in Spanish from Middlebury. Since 1994, she has been the "Dear Carol" advice columnist at *Girls' Life* Magazine. Carol and her husband, playwright Rob Ackerman, have two daughters (Lizzi and Emme) and one cat (Mike). Carol kept diaries as a girl, and her parents were writer-editors. She has taught writing at Middlebury College and created a YouTube video in English and Spanish called "Get Your Kids to Read." What will Ava do next? Find out more at CarolWeston.com.